THE DRAGON PROBLEM

THE DRAGON PROBLEM

A collaborative novel

from

Lintusen Press

The Dragon Problem
© 2024 Shawn L. Bird, editor.
Lintusen Press
ISBN: 978-1-989642-44-3 (paperback)
ISBN: 978-1-989642-45-0 (ebook)

This book uses Canadian English.

The respective chapters are copyright 2024 by the authors:
Patricia Atchison, Bonny Beswick, Isabel Cave, Abby Duncan,
Kelly Komm, Kathleen Ladislaus, Alison McBain, Robert Proudfoot,
Halli Reid, Mafalda Rose, and KT Wabick

Book cover designed by Lintusen Press with elements under license
from Canva Pro.

Lintusen Press
PO Box 10019
Salmon Arm BC
Canada V1E3B9

ABOUT
THE DRAGON PROBLEM

This book was conceived August 2023 during a workshop at When Words Collide Writers' Conference in Calgary.

The writers present brainstormed various plot elements and at the end of the workshop, authors who wished to participate in creating a collaborative novel chose the chapters they wanted to write.

Over the next several months, the authors added chapters and observations to a collaborative online document and the book grew. They worked together to craft a cohesive and entertaining story that you now hold in your hands.

Welcome to The Dragon Problem.

THE DRAGON PROBLEM

CHAPTER ONE:

wherein
Gerdty the wise woman
is thoroughly done with dragons

KATHLEEN LADISLAUS

The villagers looked skyward as Susie, a golden dragon, flew perilously low, careening over rooftops. A few golden scales fell off her ancient body as she plummeted groundward. In recent weeks, this was a daily event. Gerdty was the village wise woman. Both her magic and her healing herb garden had taken severe damage from Susie's repeated crash landings. A dragon is a fierce being when agitated, and so is Gerdty. The situation did not bode well for the village, the dragon, and the wise woman. A solution to the dragon problem was needed. For centuries, Susie and the village had co-existed in harmony. An unspoken agreement existed. In exchange for the odd meal of a sheep or cow, the dragon would shed one precious, highly valued golden scale as payment. Since the dragon slept for long periods, it could be as long as a decade between Susie taking a meal and a lucky villager obtaining a dragon scale. Now, it was occurring daily. At this rate, how long before Susie became scaleless? Have you ever seen a naked, scaleless dragon? Not an image easily erased from the mind!

Now, Gerdty may not be able to spew fire, but that day, you would have sworn smoke blew from her nostrils as she marched from her cottage toward her garden and Susie. Roland, Gerdty's husband of more than a half-century, dared not stop his wife from confronting the dragon. He stood safely inside the cottage and watched his wife set off to war against the dragon.

Gerdty walked over the smashed wooden fence with nothing but a broom for a weapon and fierce determination. Both hands tightly gripped the broom handle as she swung it to beat the dragon's backside. Gerdty exhausted herself, repeatedly smacking Susie with the broom. Dragons are stubborn sorts. You can't budge them if they don't want to move. Susie continued to root around in the herbs, ignoring Gerdty. The golden beast could have harmed the wise woman with minimal effort but refrained. Who is foolish enough to beat a dragon with a broom?

"Get out, you old lizard. Go, shoo!"

Susie ignored Gerdty.

A horrendous stench emanated from the dragon.

"You've ruined my garden," Gerdty shrieked.

Susie continued to ignore the old woman.

Gerdty "tsked" and stomped back to her cottage, raising her arms for emphasis. Mumbling under her breath, "How am I supposed to make Princess Viisi's headache potion now?"

Roland met her on the path. He had donned his blood-stained butchers' apron and held his leather roll of butcher knives and cleavers in his hand. Forced out of retirement now that Gerdty's once thriving business as a healer was seemingly at an end, he would travel the countryside peddling his services.

"So sorry about your garden, love," Roland said, bending down to kiss Gerdty on the cheek. "I'll be back in a week or so, hopefully with money enough to keep us fed."

"A golden scale would suffice to keep us. Go take one off that insufferable lizard," Gerdty huffed.

Roland knew too well there was no calming his wife. He headed for the barn to fetch his horse and cart.

The wails of a crying child in the village reached Gerdty's ears. Someone had been hurt. She was comforted knowing she still had dried herbs and salves to heal the injured. You needed fresh herbs for internal medicines, and who wanted herbs smashed and coated in dragon slobber? Unless dragon saliva had healing properties, the Dragon's Bane was ruined.

Princess Viisi suffered terrible migraine headaches. Gerdty's sure-fire cure was freshly picked Dragon's Bane brewed with sassafrass leaves. The princess became quite agitated during a headache. The pain would set her off on tirades and declarations of social change. The princess had a headache going on for two weeks now. That is when Susie began her daily assault on Gerdty's garden.

Someone was running up the flagstone path from the village to Gerdty's. It was the recent arrival to the village of Zos, Milly, the dentist.

What did she want?

CHAPTER TWO:

wherein
sacrifices
have to be made

ALISON MCBAIN

Alexander didn't expect this day to turn out the way it did. But he also didn't expect the first thing he would see in the morning when opening his eyes was old lady Charlotte. She was leaning over him in his cot and poking him in the shoulder to wake him.

Charlotte had a mean squint that was not the best way to wake up, but facing it first thing was more energizing than a cold bucket of water thrown on him. He scooched up in his bed to get away from her punishingly sharp finger, pulling his blankets up as he went. The last thing he wanted was to expose any more body parts to her sharp finger.

"Are you *pure*, boy?" she spat out.

Also not the first question he expected from her. He rubbed his eyes, as if to make the sight of the crochety old woman disappear. But when he took his hands away— nope, she was still there.

"Um... yes?" he replied.

"That's it! You heard him, folks," she shouted over her shoulder as a whole group of villagers trooped into his small cottage. Numerous hands grabbed his arms and legs and ankles, he realized that this was the one time in his life he probably should have told a lie. But it was hard to think on your feet when you weren't even *on* your feet yet.

The group included Gerdty, the wise woman. She wasn't manhandling him, but her arms were crossed and she was glaring hard enough to pop a blood vessel. She hadn't liked him since she'd caught him stealing some herbs from her garden.

He felt it was unfair that she still held a grudge. At the time, he'd just been a boy, and had been dared to steal as a prank! It was shortly after he'd been orphaned at the age of seven, and his aunt in the village had taken him in. He'd been trying to impress the other boys, who didn't seem too keen on having him show up. Perhaps they'd seen him as competition initially, because they kept daring him to do harder and harder tasks to prove he really belonged.

First, it was to fill milkmaid Marianne's boots with mud. He hadn't liked to do it—she had a lovely voice that he liked to listen to when she walked around the village, softly singing to herself. But he'd done it to see if the boys would like him and accept him.

When they heard Marianne shrieking about her boots, the boys had all fallen on the ground, laughing. But if Alexander hoped that his one task would prove him worthy to join their ranks, he was sorely mistaken.

"Not so fast, *Small*exander," said the ringleader of the group, a large boy by the name of Jack. He had a perpetual sneer on his face, and Alexander was actually sort of afraid of him. But better to be at the right hand of the devil...

Jack continued with, "We have *standards*, you know. You think you can be one of us after doing just one small thing? No, you've got a ways to go."

The next task Jack set him was nicking apples from Charlotte's prized apple orchard. The boys ate them up and left him nothing—laughing as they tossed the cores at him while he ducked. Charlotte had never caught him, but he'd confessed to all his crimes when Gerdty *did* catch him. His aunt's pinch on his ear had guaranteed it.

Stealing the herbs was the last task, and it had ended the whole escapade for him. When he saw the boys laughing at his plight, it had also put paid to his belief that they would never become his friends. No, they'd just been looking for a chump to amuse them. His aunt had walloped him good for everything he'd done, and he hadn't been able to sit down for days.

After that, he stopped trying to impress anyone. That included the girls in town, who shunned him anyway. They were always flirting with the bullies who'd gotten him in trouble. And he didn't mind so much most of the time. He just kept his head down, worked hard, and vowed to never pull a prank or tell a lie again.

When his aunt passed away last year, he'd taken over her place and continued to do odd jobs in the village— gathering and splitting firewood for the elderly, making deliveries from the businesses in town to their customers outside of town, whitewashing fences—basically, anything that would take in a few coins and keep him fed.

But he pretty much kept to himself otherwise. You'd never see him down at the local pub, trying to buddy up with the boys—now young men—who'd been his tormenters.

While it had seemed like a good strategy at the time—work hard, keep his head down, and avoid everyone—he could see now how the idea could backfire. As he was carried outside in his nightshirt, still clutching his blanket in his hands, he knew the people in the village thought he was completely expendable. Now they were planning on feeding him to the dragon.

Susie, he suddenly remembered. That was the dragon's name. She was a tough old creature and had co-existed peacefully with the village for centuries. He'd never given her much thought until recently because she only came to the village once a decade or so. Before her recent visits this past week, Alexander had only seen her once, shortly after he came to the village. At the time, he'd still been sad about his parents, and wanted nothing more than to throw himself into the dragon's path and end it all. Find his parents again in the afterlife, not stay with this cold, distant aunt he'd never met before.

But he'd been too scared. Susie had been larger than

life, a shining, golden creature out of myth and legend. When she descended onto the farmlands outside of town, he hadn't even had the courage to go closer, as some of the more daring children and adults would do. Instead, his only glimpse of her had been from his aunt's cottage window. All he'd been able to see of her was a tiny golden figure with flapping wings flying down in the distance. Then, after about a quarter of an hour, a much slower golden speck had flown off. Presumably, she'd eaten the farm animal the villagers had left out for her (usually, it was an old, slow cow—one meant for the butcher's block anyway), and perhaps, if they were lucky, left a golden scale in its place to keep the village prosperous.

Now, it seemed Alexander would get a much closer look at the dragon. Much, *much* closer. Since, from what he heard from the villagers carrying him, it seemed he was about to be fed to Susie in place of the normal livestock.

This wasn't really the place to ask why they'd chosen him. From the goings-on of the other youth his age, he knew they didn't have a lot of virgins to choose from. And the legends stated that the surest way of ending a dragon's terrorizing of a human settlement was to offer a virgin as a special treat. Sort of like a cheese platter or hors d'oeuvres.

He didn't bother to struggle. There were too many of them and he had a feeling that he had a better chance to reason with the dragon than with the villagers. They seemed hellbent on their mission.

When he saw Susie as they carried him closer, he could tell why. She had a couple of bald patches on her side where several golden scales had dropped off. As he watched, he saw another one clunk to the ground as she spun around at the villagers' approach.

The group paused before getting too close. Someone had brought some rope (didn't someone *always* bring rope to these things?) and tied his ankles and wrists together before proceeding. Someone else snatched his blanket ("Hey! Give that back!") and he guessed this was it for him.

The group deposited him about twenty feet away from the dragon and then retreated.

Susie the dragon approached him, and he hoped he wouldn't embarrass himself. But the villagers hadn't let him use the chamber pot before taking him here, so he was having a hard time with his full bladder.

Up close, he could see even more of the signs of age and wear on the once-mighty dragon. Her wings drooped and her eyes were lusterless and dull. They blinked at him, and he felt a tiny bit of kinship with her. No one wanted *her* around either, did they? If she disappeared and never came back, the villagers might be sad at the lost income but they'd not really mourn her.

He felt sympathetic and hopeful. "It's okay, Susie," he murmured quietly, for her ears alone. The villagers, who were standing a safe distance off, wouldn't hear. "We're sort of the same, aren't we?" He reached up his bound hands to touch her nose, which had descended to nudge him lying there. There was some vague idea that he could just establish some sort of connection with her, and then she would go away. Perhaps he could be the hero. After this, the villagers wouldn't ever look at him the same way again—they'd respect him into their midst. "Alexander, dragon-tamer!" he pictured them calling him.

That was his last thought before Susie opened her mouth and quickly closed it around him.

Okay, so perhaps I was wrong, he thought as Susie's jaw opened and closed several times. He thrashed, trying to breathe each time the dragon's mouth opened and air rushed in. But his face, his body, everything was coated by a thick layer of dragon saliva.

After a moment, he realized that there wasn't really any pain. He'd sort of expected getting eaten alive would hurt. And he thought perhaps it might be a bit faster too—he was still being tossed around in the dragon's mouth, with not much progress being made going farther down the creature's gullet.

All of a sudden, the world turned upside down and he was tumbling through the air. Sky, ground, sky, ground, thud!

The wind was knocked out of him and he struggled to breathe. Meanwhile, his hands instinctually went up to his face and scrabbled at the mucus preventing him from seeing and breathing. He took a great gasp of air as the sludge dripped off from him, and blinked a couple of times.

He was just in time to glance up and see the dragon spread her wings in a clap of sound like thunder and launch herself into the air. Even after being a failed appetizer, he marvelled at the beauty of the sight of her as the sun glistened off her shining scales that twinkled and shone like a million gems. She was breathtaking even now, and he could see why humans would rather appease this dangerous creature than kill her. There was something amazing about her, despite the fear she could bring to the surface.

He scraped the dragon saliva off as best he could. He shook his still-bound hands. The smell was simply atrocious. Did the dragon never hear of a toothbrush?

The villagers who had carried him to the dragon approached him. Many seemed a bit sheepish at their failed attempt to sacrifice him to the dragon. One of them produced a knife—it was someone he hadn't seen in the original crowd. Marianne, the milkmaid with the beautiful voice. The one who knew he'd filled her boots with mud when they were both kids.

She cut the rope around his hands and ankles and afterward wiped her dirty hands on the grass to clean them. Then she turned on the crowd who'd carried him out to the dragon. "For shame!" she told them, and Alexander felt a burgeoning of hope in his chest. Here was at least one person sticking up for him, even though she didn't have to at all. "What did Alexander ever do to you?"

She knew his name! *Wow*, he thought.

The crowd muttered, kicked at the dirt in embarrassment, and then drifted off to their own cottages.

"Thank you," Alexander said to Marianne.

She shrugged and looked away. "I'm sorry I wasn't here earlier to stop them," she said. Then she turned back to him. "Are you okay?"

He grinned. There was nothing holding him to this village except habit and familiarity. However, the familiar wasn't always good, as evidenced by what the villagers had tried to do to him.

"You know what?" he said. "I am. Thank you again. I hope that you can help solve the village's problem. You have a good heart, so you might be the only one who can." He stood up and brushed at himself one more time, although his actions were not really helping much. But he had plenty of soap in his cottage that he'd made, and he would take a bracing bath in the nearby lake before he left.

Marianne watched him limp away—the fall had been a bit hard—but he didn't bother looking back.

After he was clean again and dressed—having thrown away his dragon-spit-covered nightshirt—he packed up as many of his belongings as would fit into his small farm cart and hitched up his only donkey to pull it. No one stopped by or said anything, and to that he was glad.

No one here cared if he lived or died. Since his aunt's death—no, further back than that—since his parents' death, he'd just been barely surviving. It was facing being eaten by a dragon that had made him realize he didn't belong in this village. He never had. He'd always been an outsider.

By the time the sun set on this day, he was far away from the village that had tried to kill him.

He'd never been happier in his life.

CHAPTER THREE:

wherein
the kid
is not all right

ALISON MCBAIN

W<i>here the heck has he gone now?</i> thought Kimberly, frantically running outside.

She was often worried about her youngest son, Samuel Junior. It seemed that every time she turned around, he'd gone wandering off on his own. He was only five years old, and he was always turning up in odd places—down at the cow byre, over in the schoolhouse, and sometimes even across town at Grandma Gerdty's. No matter how many times she scolded him for going off by himself, he never seemed to listen.

Just like his father, Kimberly thought with a roll of her eyes. Her husband had a bad habit of wandering too, sometime right over to another woman's bedchamber. But he always wandered back, so it was hard for her to complain. He provided well enough for their family of seven, and that was better than some in the town. Her friend Zella, for example, hadn't seen her own husband in five years.

And she's much happier for it, said a little voice in the back of Kimberly's head, but she ignored it. Much easier not to think about a life completely on her own, even if she tended to fly solo most of the time anyway.

Needless to say, there wasn't much help from Samuel Senior when it came to the kids. And, to be honest, he rarely helped care for their small plot of land too. She was the one who got up before the crack of dawn, milked and fed the cows and goats, fed the chickens, nursed the baby, got the children ready for school, and then did her piecework all day long to sell for a few extra coins. Any money she earned went to pay for schoolbooks, as well as any other necessities for the children and herself.

By the time she fed her five children at night and had

them all in bed, she would fall asleep in the quiet of the evening, sometimes sitting upright in the rocking chair by the fire. She'd wake up with a start when the door slammed open—Sam Sr. coming home from wherever he'd been.

When he came home, he would always have his arms full of the richest of things that you could imagine. Everything from crates of the finest glass mirrors, bolts of velvet, and boxes of uncut jewels. He would sell these items at the palace or to nearby noble houses, and then give her some of the coin to pay for their daily needs. She had no idea where the rest of the money went, but she had a strong suspicion that it was spent at the local pub or on the women he seemed so fond of. Or perhaps he invested it in buying more goods, if he was actually buying the luxury items and not obtaining them some other way.

She didn't want to ask. Money was money. Even if she asked, she greatly doubted he would tell her if he were doing something illicit.

So, when the banging door woke her, often around midnight, she would stumble upright in shock before she was truly awake and be heading for the table to serve her husband. He would sit at the table while she dipped up a spoonful of stew from the pot that was always hanging over the fire, and she would serve it to him on a trencher of bread—he would often be hungry after his long days away. She would also pour a cup of mead and leave the bottle on the table for him before heading off to bed.

Sometimes he would join her in the bed under the covers; sometimes not. She actually preferred when he just came home, dropped off his goods and coins, ate, and then left again. The silence after he departed would lull her back to sleep, and the bed was often too small for the both of them to rest comfortably. He would often hog both the space and the quilt, and she would curl up in a small ball to stay warm and sleep fitfully until it was time to wake in the morning for her daily chores.

But at times like today, with Samuel Junior missing, Kimberly wished she had a second set of eyes to help her. She'd been nursing the baby and just turned her back on Samuel for one moment, but then he was nowhere to be found when she went looking for him. Considering the front door was slightly ajar—he never closed it behind him—she could guess that he'd taken her distraction and made a run for it.

She strapped the baby to her back and then took off to

check Samuel's usual hiding places. The stone cow byre out back? She looked under and round the cows and behind the bales of hay, but there weren't that many places to hide. Next, she walked by the stream—Samuel liked to hunt for frogs. While the stream wasn't deep enough to be dangerous, it was definitely deep enough for wet feet. However, he wasn't there either and there were no small footprints in the soft mud of the bank.

Perhaps down by the school? Samuel always wanted to be doing what his older siblings were doing, but they considered him a terrible pest. She couldn't remember the number of times she heard: "Mom, Samuel followed me to school *again!*" He was too young to go yet, according to the law of the land, but sometimes the teacher would make a place for him to sit and listen to the lessons, which he seemed to enjoy. At least it kept him quiet and out of trouble.

She was just headed there when a sound made her look up.

Before the past month, it'd been years since the dragon had disturbed their quiet life in town. Kimberly had been nearly a child herself the last time Susie had been fed her livestock tribute before heading back to her hidden cave in the mountains.

But after these past few weeks, there was no mistaking what that whooshing sound through the air was—the beat of the dragon's wings. And there was especially no mistaking that thunderous roar, which they'd heard quite often of late.

And Kimberly couldn't help but feel a pit yawning in her stomach that the dragon was approaching and Samuel was nowhere to be found.

She couldn't run while carrying the baby, but she hurried as fast as she could over to Gerdty's place. Perhaps her mother would have some trick for finding her missing son, or perhaps Samuel had taken the initiative and made his way over to his grandmother's. Either way, she had to do *something*.

The sound of wingbeats grew louder. In fact, they seemed to be following her. She glanced behind her and saw that Susie was flying in from the mountains at Kimberly's back, growing closer with each wingbeat. It seemed like they were headed in the same direction, and Kimberly wondered if that were so. Her mother had told her about the destruction of her garden by the foul creature, so why would Susie want to return to the scene of the crime? There wasn't any more damage she could possibly do.

But that seemed to be the dragon's destination as she swooped by overhead. Kimberly could see her mother's cottage up ahead, her father shaking a rake at the dragon as Susie landed in the ruins of her mother's garden.

Kimberly's hurrying footsteps slowed, but it was out of relief—there wasn't any glimpse of Samuel in Gerdty's yard. *Phew.* He might be adventurous, but there was no way that he would approach a full-sized dragon. He'd be scared out of his mind.

That didn't solve the mystery of where he was, though. Kimberly dithered in the road. Susie appeared to be talking to her dad, Roland. He'd stopped shaking his rake, but she could tell he wasn't happy by the hunched posture of his back.

Now, here came the big question—should Kimberly go near Susie with little Emma strapped to her back? Or should she wait for the dragon to leave again before asking for her mother's help in finding Samuel?

Susie reared back on her legs and threw her head in the air. A roar escaped her throat, as well as an ashy stream of fire that spurted straight up in the air. "If you will not help me, I will find someone who will!" she shouted. The breeze from her yelling blew off Roland's hat, which Gerdty neatly caught, since she was standing behind her husband. She handed him back his hat, and he jammed it onto his head with a huff.

"That is your choice," Gerdty said in her loud, carrying voice. "Even if I wanted to help you, I could not. You've destroyed my garden and trampled on the remains. The only thing that's useful anymore are these." She picked up a small scale that had dropped off Susie's skin when she roared. "But you better be careful, girlie. You lose many more of these, and you're toast."

"Toast?" Susie appeared confused.

"Finis. Caput. Dead." For good measure, Gerdty drew a finger across her throat and made the "ksssk" sound.

Susie's eyes seemed to widen in shock. "You dare to threaten me?"

"No, you idiot dragon." Gerdty shook her head. "Your scales are what sustains your fire. You lose your fire, you won't live very long."

Susie pawed at the ground in agitation. Kimberly figured she'd waited long enough at a distance and hurried up to her parents. But when Gerdty saw her only daughter, she scowled.

"You shouldn't be here, Kim—get back."

"I can't," Kimberly said. While she wasn't so foolish to step between her parents and Susie, she came as close as she dared. "Samuel's missing."

"Missing?" Gerdty whipped around to look at Susie. "Hey, you old snake! Did you have anything to do with my grandson disappearing?"

Susie's anger seemed to disappear. "Your grandson? I have seen no grand person."

"A boy," Gerdty clarified, enunciating each word. "He is a little boy."

The dragon shook her head at the same time that Kimberly said, "He was already gone by the time Susie showed up. I don't think she's responsible."

"I am not responsible!" roared the dragon, rearing back again to spit fire into the air. "How dare you..."

Gerdty pshawed her. "Get going, then. I have nothing to help you with." She crossed her arms and glared.

Susie got the hint. Or half of it, at least. She spread wide her jaws and scooped up a big mouthful of the remaining herbs in Gerdty's garden into her jaws. With a mouthful of medicinal plants, she spread her wings and began to flap. Kimberly was pushed back a step by the force of the wind, and baby Emma began to howl and flail on her back.

"Mama!" she heard over the wail of the growing wind as Susie gained the air. Horrified, she turned and saw Samuel. He was running straight for her, his arms outstretched. He'd been hiding on the far side of the garden, over by the brambles.

"No, Samuel!" she shouted, but it was too late.

The force of flapping to ascend had loosened one more scale from Susie's side. This one, though, was not small like the last one. It was the size of Kimberly's outstretched hand and made of thick, solid gold. It came plummeting down from the sky at a terrible velocity, and Kimberly screamed as she saw it on a collision course right where Samuel was running.

It struck him, and he went down. She was already rushing over to his suddenly still form sprawled out on the ground, his body lying in the hollow where Susie had rested and compressed the ground beneath her. The weight of a dragon was to be reckoned with, not just because of her large size but her incredibly heavy gold scales.

One of which had knocked her son out cold. Perhaps killed him.

Kimberly found herself on her hands and knees, bending over Samuel. He seemed so still and pale, a gash of blood on his forehead, that she feared the worst. Was he... dead?

She leaned over to rest her cheek near his wide-open mouth. The faintest breath touched her face like a healing balm, and she leaned back and covered her mouth with her hands as tears filled her eyes. He was alive!

Her father helped her carry the unconscious Samuel back to her house, and he put her son into his bed. "Should I wait with you?" her dad asked with a heavy tone.

She shook her head, the tears falling down her cheeks. "We'll be okay," she said, and it was half to reassure herself. "Take care of Mom."

Roland pressed one hand to her shoulder as she fell to her knees before her son's bed and took both of his hands in hers. Her dad meant the gesture as a comfort, but she only felt empty. She heard the quiet click of the front door as her dad headed out.

There was only one thing left for her to do. Anger swirled through her at the unjust nature of what had happened to her child, quickly followed by a burgeoning rage against that heartless and cruel dragon who had nearly killed her son. Kimberly had to focus on one thing at a time, though, and there was no room for anger in the endless void of her aching heart.

Revenge on the monstrous dragon would have to wait. There was only one thing she could do, and one thing only. She bent her head and prayed for the life of her child.

CHAPTER FOUR:

wherein
dental drama
ensues

ABBY DUNCAN

Shoshan, or Susie, as the villagers called her, unfurled her glittery gold wings and leapt into the air, gliding gracefully along in the warm wind currents. The balmy breeze felt loving, like a second home, and Susie hummed a satisfied song as she flew in the late afternoon sky. The scent of floral blooms, honey and blackberries accented the sweet air.

Finally on her return path home to her treasured remote mountain peak, she hoped she would finally have some well-earned rest.

The yarrow and peppermint she'd snatched from Gerdty's garden eased the aching deep in Susie's maw. Buckets of dragon drool dripped out the numb side of her mouth, sloshing down her neck and into the sky below her.

Hopefully, some of that drool would drop on that horrid dentist. The last time she'd seen Milly, that horrible human tried to remove her tooth. Shoshan smelled Milly's malevolent intentions and refused to permit the extraction. She knew full well it was simply a goat's horn stuck deep in her grizzled gums.

No matter how many times Milly tried to gaslight her.

With each visit to the terrible tooth torturer, her condition worsened. Sadly, Susie did not have any other options. Dr. Sanchez refused to treat her at all. And she'd angered Gerdty too much to convince her to reach into her enormous mouth and try to pull out the horn.

Milly kept testing her, repeatedly gauging her reaction to different poultices and numbing concoctions. She shuddered with how close she'd come to accidentally roasting Hilary, Milly's assistant, after an errant sneeze.

Hilary was forgiving, and fortunately, no permanent damage was done.

That was only the start of Shoshan's problems. She'd lost some larger scales off her hindquarters, leaving her skin exposed, dry, and itchy. Her leathery skin was prickling in places she could not reach to scratch.

As if the thought alone summoned it, the crawling sensation returned. With nothing else to focus on, Susie dropped and spun back toward the village in search of a dragon sized boulder or outcropping to scratch on.

After an hour of searching, a sneeze sent Susie's errant flight spiralling, and without her once youthful reflexes, she crashed into one side of a large red barn.

Splintered wood, hay and feathers shot into the early-evening air. Several chickens squawked in annoyance; a cacophony of disgruntled bleating and mooing came from the other side of the barn. Nosing through the rubble, she sighed in relief. She could not smell any blood in the collapsed remains of that part of the barn. She preferred live cows and goats to eating them a la plancha, anyway.

Farmer William shot out his back door, hollering vitriol containing several unrepeatable words at the ancient being. "You had a large empty field to choose from, and you land on top of my brand-new barn? Can't you see I just finished painting it, you overgrown salamander?" He stumbled over his own shoes as he attempted to adjust his stained overalls and smooth down his riotous greying curls.

"Are you old, useless, or simply stupid, Susie?"

Susie growled, feeling the fire crawl up her throat, and breathed smoke out her giant nostrils. She reminded herself that humans were stringy and tasted awful. They caused indigestion something terrible and seemed to get quite upset if you roasted them indiscriminately. However, William was tempting her to try snacking on a human yet again. Promise or not.

Instead, she spun toward him, letting her giant tail swish in the air behind her, and bared her teeth in warning. "I did not intend to harm you or your barn, young one," Susie rumbled, arching her long neck to her majestic full height. She quite hoped he didn't hear the arthritic popping when she did so.

William remembered himself. After all, he was screeching at a being who could easily swallow him in a single gulp. "Well, yes. Of course, you wouldn't want to do that to me. After all, you have always had a good trade deal with my father, and his father before him. It would be quite the shame to end such a profitable relationship by damaging my barn further." William pulled a wooden stool from the standing portion of the barn with his small, pudgy paw, and sat upon it, arms folded.

Susie nodded her enormous head and folded her wings forward around her. If this William intended to harm her, she would be the end of him.

"Susie, I am sorry. I should not have yelled at you in that manner or spoken to you in the way I did. Please forgive me." William's words contradicted his tone. Shoshan may be two thousand years old and no longer had her once-keen eyesight. But her hearing was as keen as ever.

Susie narrowed her eyes and nodded her serpentine head and returned the pleasantries. This was the way William's great grandfather used to address her. Shoshan appreciated such a familiar cadence; however, she did not drop her guard.

Humans revealed much more of their true selves in anger than they ever did in pretty, enchanting speeches.

Tamping down the fire, she replied, "It is forgiven. Tread carefully, human. I am not easily deceived."

The flare of William's nostrils spoke volumes. Yes, this small man was angry, down to his very soul. His body projected a weak aura, thin and muddled with red streaks of anger.

"As you should also tread lightly. Your welcome is waning with all the damage you've caused in Zos. This is so unlike you and your reputation. Yes, you occasionally feed from our livestock, but you pick the lamest animals. This is most appreciated, I might say." Once again, William's words dripped in derision.

Susie snorted some smoke in William's general direction, wishing he would get to the point of his farce of an inquiry. Of course, she would engage in the niceties, such as they were. After all, dragons love tradition.

Glancing behind him, she could tell, even with her failing eyesight that his farm was falling into disrepair. The supposed new barn smelled of rot. His wooden fence lining the pasture was crumbling in several places, and worst of all, the once-majestic farmhouse. It listed to one side, the shingles drooping in the centre. What was once a grand farmhouse full of life and children now lay empty. The only noise, apart from William's wheezy breath, was the livestock in the barn.

"Tell me, William... are you the last of your line?" Susie rumbled, allowing her voice to echo across the property.

"Are you all that remains of a once great family?"

William ticked, and a bitter scent emanated from his form. "Not the last. My youngest brother has three children, two boys, who will take over from me when I die. What about your family, Susie? What are dragon families like?"

Susie tilted her head to one side, drawing closer to William. "It's been two millennia since I last saw what you would call my family. We are strictly solitary creatures. Once we hatch, and we can feed and defend ourselves, our family will leave us in our solitude."

William smiled, his aura lightened and swirled with streaks of green. "Then you and I are very similar, Susie. My father passed away when I was still young. And my mother passed a few years after. I was barely old enough to shave when I started running this farm. And look how well it is doing now!"

Susie nodded politely, unsure if William intended his rhetoric to be ironic. His home was clearly crumbling around him. However, it would be rude to point that out.

The first stars appeared in the sky, and sniffing, Shoshan could tell if she did not depart soon, she could not use the now-cooling currents to carry her home.

Instead, she delicately removed a small golden scale from her tail, not much larger than a human's eye, and slid it to William, paying her debt for the damage to his home.

Before William could protest, she could smell his derision. She took to the sky, ending any attempt at debate.

The dark sky and cool winds made it difficult for Shoshan to find her path. She twisted herself around, looking for the waterfall that marked the path to her peak, and caught the edge of her wing on an errant tree branch. Sent spiralling, she tumbled through the air, dropping like a stone until she finally crashed into a small patch of herbs and flowers. Screaming in frustration at her aching wing, a ball of fire hit the nearby fence, setting it aflame.

It was then she realized where she was. Yet again, she'd damaged Gerdty's garden. And she'd set a fire. Again. There were not enough dragon scales in the world to calm Gerdty when she was ready for a row.

Gerdty's indignant grumbling echoed from a room in the nearby homestead, and a light came on. Knowing her way from here, Susie took to the sky to escape the wrath of the angry alchemist.

Pins and needles shot down her wing to her

dewclaws, and she grunted in frustration. She knew exactly what she needed to do to make amends with Gerdty. She only hoped she was not yet beyond gaining her old friend's forgiveness, and that Gerdty would appreciate the treasure that Shoshan planned to share.

CHAPTER FIVE:

wherein
Milly the Dentist
manipulates more than teeth

HALLI REID

"**Your Four o'clock is here.**" The receptionist's voice over the intercom carried a slight tremble. "Hilary, I hope you're ready?"

"We are," I said. We all knew who the four o'clock really was. Accommodations had been made.

I watched the massive beast duck under the lights, casting passing shadows and creaking scales with every thunderous step. I was speechless, but the dentist, my boss, seemed unimpressed.

"Maintenance literally had to take the door off its hinges to fit you in." Dr. Mildred scowled as the beast tried squeezing her lizard-like bulk into the exam room without knocking anything over.

"I know," Susie mumbled. "I really appreciate you fitting me in."

"Don't get too happy. Keep your tail still." Dr. Mildred watched as the dragon gingerly moved into place. When she turned her back to me, the dentist kicked my stool, making me totter precariously on two wobbly legs. "Be careful, Susie!" her blame came out as a bark.

"I'm sorry," Susie apologized, "I didn't even notice."

"It's fine." I caught Dr. Mildred Mandible's death glare which told me to play along. I kept my job because I was so adept at playing along. The corruption went beyond this office.

"How can you notice anything with those massive scales?" she said. "No wonder you are such a hazard."

The insults were compounded when we traded our regular masks and gloves for heavy duty equipment. Dr. Mildred donned a welder's mask and thick, leather gloves. She huffed in annoyance with every movement so Susie could notice multiple times how inconvenient her existence was.

"Now, be careful this time. Open slowly. We don't want to lose our eyebrows again. Right Hilary?" She turned to me with her death glare, and I nodded in agreement. "Fire extinguisher ready?" she asked.

"Ready." I put my thumb on the pin and pulled myself up closer.

"That stuff tastes awful," Susie said.

"Do you want your tooth fixed or not?" Mildred asked.

"I suppose," Susie replied. She slowly opened her vast maw full of enamel machetes. Like a portal to hell, her cavernous throat expanded before me, already red with heat.

"Aim right to the back," the dentist directed me. To the dragon she said, "Say Ahhh!"

Susie complied.

The sound of rushing flames sent me into a panic. I also said "Ahhh!" in the tradition of facing a life-threatening firebolt to the face. I shoved my arms into the hot hiss of dragon breath and past the rows of lethal fangs. With strength beyond logic, I whipped off the pin and pulled the trigger.

The sweet release of white foam shot from the canister and into the dragon's throat. It sprayed over the glowing embers in her mouth and doused them instantly. Some foam came flying back in my face but I stayed in position until every drop was used. Susie gagged and splashed white foam over the floor and over me.

When she could breathe again her voice came garbled through a filled mouth, "Next time could you use a fire hose?"

Dr. Mildred said nothing but went straight to work. She used a hammer and chisel to knock on each tooth and gouge into each crevice and groove. Susie tried to say, "It's the one in the back." But it sounded more like, "Ida unuhdu ack."

"This one?" Dr. Mildred shoved her torso into the lizard mouth and banged the hammer.

"Yow!" Susie screamed.

I was prepared with a second canister and dosed her mouth again as a measure of safety. Dr. Mildred was in the way and she emerged from the mouth wiping foam off her visor. Death glare number three.

"Sorry." I shrugged.

She ignored my apology. "Susie, that tooth is close to cinders," she diagnosed. "There's only so much heat enamel can handle. It's an issue for dragons your age. A design flaw in your evolution." She continued to wipe foam out of her hair and off of her collar.

"I've had these teeth for thousands of years," Susie mumbled through the foam.

"I'll have to get some specialized equipment. It will cost you." She tapped the tooth again, making the dragon wince. Lifting the visor on her mask, she enunciated her words. "Unless you're willing to do me another favor."

The request lingered in the air while the dentist wrote some notes. After a long pause Susie spoke up. "What sort of favor?"

With her bulky gloves Mildred continued to scribble on her clipboard. "My electoral competition has been giving me some grief."

"Dr. Sanchez?" Susie asked.

I knew where this conversation was going, and I tried to change the subject. "Should I contact the arborist to borrow his tree spade? Unless we want to save the gums."

"A jackhammer will work best." Mildred's death glares were constant today, sending my heart into palpitations. Still, I was pretty sure I wouldn't get fired. At least not when she had this preoccupation with becoming mayor. She needed all minions on deck.

"What do you need from me this time?" Susie asked.

"I need you to take care of him for me," Mildred said.

"In what way?" Susie's scaly face wore an apprehensive expression.

Mildred huffed. "Dispatch him. Do I have to spell it out?" Her gloved hands slapped the clipboard.

Another long pause filled the room as Susie processed this statement. "Why?" she asked.

Mildred groaned. "Why wouldn't you? The biggest part of his campaign is banishing you. He called you vermin! I'm the only candidate who welcomes you as a member of society. I'm the one calling for equality. If you want to keep your cave I have to win the election and you know it." Mildred gave me the signal to rinse out the foam, so I grabbed the hose and vacuum.

Susie put up a paw to stop me. "But why do I have to kill him?"

Mildred's eyes widened. "Oh my God, Susie! Why do you care? You've lost count of how many people you've killed. What's one more?"

Susie cast her eyes down. "That was a long time ago." Her voice trailed off.

"Dragons don't lose their touch. It's muscle memory. Unless your age makes you incapable, in which case what good are you?" Mildred turned up her nose in disgust.

Susie spat the foam in a huge gob all over the wall, and in the same movement, shot out her , clamping it around Mildred's neck. With her thumb she popped off the welder's mask like the head of a dandelion, then she placed her thumb under Mildred's chin, ready to pop her head off in the same manner. "You're right. It is muscle memory. And my age doesn't matter in terms of killing skills." Susie leaned forward, smoke seeping from her nostrils. "But it does matter to my career. I'm trying to enjoy a peaceful retirement."

Mildred waited for the dragon's grip to ease a bit so she could talk. "We have a business transaction here. Nothing more. Do you want to do business or not?"

Susie took a deep breath, closing her eyes and opening them again. If Mildred's death glare was effective, Susie's was terrifying. She held the dentist's throat for another minute before relaxing and slowly removing her paw. "I'll think about it." The dragon wiped the remaining foam from her maw.

"I'll book the specialized equipment and schedule the extraction when I receive your payment. My receptionist will contact you." The dentist handed me her gloves and apron. "Clean up this mess," she directed. Without a backward glance she exited the room.

Realizing I was now alone in the room with a grumpy, fire-breathing monster I jumped into action. I grabbed the mop and furiously wiped the walls.

Susie shook her head and squeezed herself carefully out the door.

I let out the air I was holding in. I wasn't sure who I was more afraid of: my boss and mob leader, Dr. Mildred Mandible or the ancient titan with a toothache. Yes, the dragon had burned villages, eaten livestock, and instilled fear in the hearts of mankind for centuries, but what kind of person had the guts to blackmail said monster for their own personal gain? Susie was facing an enemy she never had before. Something entirely new. Not only the unstoppable progress of aging and the pain that went with it, but the exploitation of that pain.

I was impressed by Mildred's capabilities in controlling a dragon, if that's what she was actually able to do. Humans had a bad track history when it came to playing with fire.

CHAPTER SIX:

wherein
Princess Viisi
has a headful of trouble

BONNY BESWICK

I **long to loosen the plaits** woven into my hair. My maid wound them so tightly my eyebrows are pulled into a look of permanent surprise.

Only a few years ago, I would have screeched and demanded a different hair style, but at the mature age of sixteen, even as the youngest of five princesses, I have learned to exhibit a modicum of decorum. Oh, but my head throbs!

Just as my place on the royal balcony is in the back

row, my place at the banquet is at the distant end of the table. Tonight, I have no appetite and am glad to be far from the focus of attention. No one notices I've hidden my greens under the stuffed squab. My stomach roils with nausea from the migraine and I dare not take even one bite of my favorite dish, the wild rice studded with toasted pecans and raisins. All I want is to go back to my chambers, free my hair, and lay my aching head on the cool pillow.

The son of a distant lord is seated next to me. He has fanciful ideas of taking my hand in marriage, no doubt encouraged by his mother who was spurned by my father when he chose my mother as his queen. Shall I crush this young man's hopes with one of my usual barbs, or should I be coquettish, as my parents would wish?

My older sisters have a heavier burden in the matters of marriage. They bear the obligation to produce royal heirs, while I am far enough down the line of succession to be free to reproduce, or not, as I and the fates determine. In truth, I only have eyes for an innocent farm boy who works the fields not far from our castle gates.

Without the pressures of succession, my future is more flexible. I may choose to be a Lady of Leisure, a mother, or even to undertake an avocation, shocking though that may seem to our subjects. My sisters will represent the crown, while I will be free to choose my own path. The route I've chosen, yet not announced even to my father, will surprise all.

The eager suitor cants his head in my direction, but I tire of his boasts of fighting the dragon and saving our town from the shadow that flies overhead. It takes no brave knight to harass the poor thing. Her vision and power of flight are failing her, and the wretch is now as much a danger to herself as to our citizenry. She has as much need of healing as anyone in this kingdom.

The emboldened youth oversteps. "Your Royal Highness, may I call you by your first name, Viisi?"

The pounding in my head, and the prisms of light at the periphery of my vision drive me to be even less politic and polite than usual. Speaking without filters, I lift my chin and stare down my nose. "You may not. I am Princess Viisi, and you will address me as such, or Your Royal Highness, should you prefer."

He blushes and stutters, the spots on his face becoming more pronounced. He is not as fortunate as I to have a balm from the Wise Woman, Gerdty, to keep my complexion clear and smooth. "My apologies, Your Royal Highness. I meant no offence."

His bravado vanishes in the same manner as do the colours of the rainbow when the sun falls below the horizon. A cone of silence falls over us and I know he now will not speak unless spoken to. Around us, the room buzzes with conversation and laughter fills the air. Across from us, a dowager and a squire spar flirtatiously, though she is twenty years his senior. 'Tis all part of courtly politics to flirt, to preen and to plot.

I gaze at the congealing butter sauce on my plate, praying for a speedy end to this tedious banquet where my father entertains the odious dentist and mayoral hopeful, Dr. Mildred "Milly to my friends" Stevenson. At the corner of my vision, a well groomed, but reddened and chapped hand reaches past me and removes the dish. I softly say, "Thank you." Unnecessary, I know, and even breaching protocol to treat the footman as anything but invisible, but our servants receive little appreciation for the work they perform.

I endure one last nauseating whiff of the squab and greens before it is replaced with a cake with fresh raspberries and warm vanilla sauce. I may be able to manage a few nibbles, even with my upset stomach.

While savoring the tart bite of fruit, I decide I have some sympathy for the boy beside me. He had no choice in where he sat, or in the demands of his parents to make a match. The future of his family likely depends upon his ability to woo me. I feel a prick of guilt that I have wounded the young lord. His embarrassment is plain to see, and I remind myself that if it is my intention to run for mayor against the corrupt Milly, I must cultivate positive relationships, nurture allies and garner votes, wherever I can.

I turn to him. "I apologize for my rudeness. I unfortunately have a beastly headache and am ill-tempered as a result. Please, you are welcome to address me as Viisi. And how shall I address you?"

He blushes an even deeper shade of crimson, but manages to stammer, "Rodney, Your Grace. Ah, Viisi."

I grit my teeth behind a gracious smile, and make light conversation with him until I overhear the courtier across from me mention Susie.

Alas, the ancient dragon who makes her home high above the kingdom in a hidden cave, has fallen afoul of one of the mayoralty candidates, Dr. Sanchez. He proposes to banish her, should he be elected. I am adamantly opposed to such an idea, as Susie is as much a part of the kingdom as any other living creature. As much as the grey wolf or tawny cougar that lurk in the forest, the dragon plays a part in the ecosystem.

I clearly, and rather forcefully, make my opinion known to those around me, until my father signals the end of the meal. At last, free to escape the stuffy and clamorous dining hall, I quickly bid the guests good night. I offer particular attention to the young Lord Rodney so he is not humiliated by my unceremonious departure, and flee through the halls to my sleeping quarters.

The cool darkness in my chambers embraces me. A small fire crackles in the fireplace, but otherwise the only light comes from the moonbeams streaming through my window. Earlier, I had dismissed my maid so I am left to relish the solitude of the night. The heavy satin brocade of my gown rustles when I settle at the dressing table and untangle my plaits. With each braid released, my dark hair bursts to an exuberant halo. My sisters have smooth dark tresses, but I am blessed with the wild riot that is my trademark, as much as my sharp tongue and willful attitude.

Moonlight pours through a crystal vial positioned on the sill. Gerdty, the wise woman who is without equal in healing arts, gave this diamond-clear liquid to me. It is made even more potent by the power of the full moon, and promises relief from my migraine.

The potion is brewed from herbs, both common and mysterious, grown in her garden. Alas, the poor dragon, Susie, while searching for a cure for her own maladies, destroyed the plot. The once powerful dragon, whether because of poor vision or fatigue, crashed into the cherished and rare plants. Until the garden regrows, Gerdty can no longer concoct her potions, and those of us who depend upon her, the villagers, dragon, and even me with my migraines, will suffer.

"Just call me Milly," the dentist, declares that my debilitating headaches are caused by my wisdom teeth. "My dear Princess Viisi," she coos, "If you would only allow me to remove those dreadful back teeth, your headaches would be no more."

I know better. I know her game. She is a thief, stealing wisdom teeth from all the mouths into which she can wiggle her worm-like fingers. In return for relieving our aches and pains, she asks for our teeth. And for money of course. She takes advantage of all, but preys most viciously on the commoners who have little freedom in their miserable lives.

My family have reigned in this kingdom for centuries, guiding and advising the local mayor and council. We have supported and encouraged Gerdty and her predecessors as the providers of healing. Unfortunately, my family has been oblivious, perhaps willingly so, to the plight of commoners. The citizenry toil and pay taxes but receive little in return, except the privilege of lining the streets to watch the pageantry of royal celebrations. I have observed their hardships and believe my family can do more for them. We must.

We can learn from our past. By virtue of my birth, I have access to secret rooms where dusty tomes are stored, perhaps even hidden from those not of royal birth. In these books and scrolls, there lies ancient knowledge, and much of it has been forgotten. Why hasn't it been passed down? Why haven't we learned from the past?

On a particularly old scroll, I found that the Ancients believed wisdom is stored in our back-most molars. These teeth erupt from the jaw later in life and are a repository of knowledge. In fact, a ceremony, one that is no longer observed, used to have the healer of a village remove these teeth at death. The teeth were ground into a powder, then mixed into draughts to enhance the abilities of the wise women. Over the millennia, this ritual has been abandoned, and the importance of the wisdom tooth has been forgotten. If we no longer carry forward the wisdom from the past, is this why we struggle and are unable to improve the plight of all citizens? Is this why we cannot bring ourselves to treat all people as equals?

Somehow, it seems that Mildred the Malevolent has learned of the power within the wisdom teeth and wishes to use it to augment her influence. Dr. Stevenson is convincing people to part with their wisdom teeth. From the glint in her eyes and the way her fingers twitch when asking to extract perfectly healthy teeth, I have no doubt she uses them for her own gain. I fear that if she becomes the new mayor, she will use this ill-gotten knowledge not to lead our people wisely, but to control them. Dictate. I believe her intention is to build an army and attempt to usurp the role my family has played for hundreds of years. I may not always agree with my father, but he governs with compassion, and our family has been benevolent. I fear Mildred will rule with cruelty and deprivation.

With the last of my braids untangled, I exchange my elaborately embroidered gown for my sleeping shift. My hair sways with my slow steps across the rug-covered stone floor. I halt in front of the window and take the vial in my hands. The potion glows with the power of moonlight, promising relief. I remove the crystal stopper and let the effervescent liquid swirl in my mouth, savouring the peppermint sharpness. Already I feel the pressure in my head easing. Like a flower opening in springtime, the bands of tension around my forehead release.

I slide beneath my blankets, letting my mind fill with kind and pleasant thoughts, plans for a gentler kingdom where all have access to the magical elixir that relieves pain. I fall into delicious sleep.

Most mornings, I bound into the breakfast room to bid good-morning to my father, The king, and my mother. Always, my mother dabs her lips with a finely embroidered linen and frowns. "Viisi, your hair?"

I invariably snap back, "Motherrrr, I have no appointments this morning so there is no need for my hair to be imprisoned by pins and ribbons."

She is unrelenting. "Still, you must make yourself

presentable."

I do not give in easily. I never have, and to be truthful, I believe mother would be disappointed if I did.

"But if no one is going to see me, why should it matter?"

"The servants will see you; courtiers and others making petitions to your father will see you. I will see you."

"But..."

"You will have your maid fix your hair, and you will don a proper gown."

I never win this argument, the one we have had every morning since I turned fourteen, when protocol dictated I don an adult form of dress and imprison my hair.

My father, reading his Royal Dispatches, rarely becomes involved in our domestic squabbles unless pressed.

This morning, however, I shock my parents. I have come to the Breakfast Room dressed in a subdued gown, and my hair contained under a wimple.

"Good morning, Father. Good morning, Mother."

My mother, even without looking at me, is ready to engage in our morning sparring. She glances up, and when she sees I am dressed appropriately, tries to hide her amazement. After an appraising pause, she says, "Good morning, Daughter."

It takes a few breaths before my father realizes the tenor of this morning's conversation is not the usual battle. He peers above the dispatch in his hands. His eyebrows lift behind the wire-rimmed spectacles, then he nonchalantly returns to his reading. He is not one to let his emotions show.

Instead of flopping into the nearest elaborately carved chair, I remain standing, hands folded primly in front of me.

"Father, Mother. May I discuss something with you?"

I wait. My father gives a single nod, indicating I should speak.

"I wish to run for mayor."

Mother returns her china cup to its saucer with nary a clink.

The king lowers his papers and peers over his spectacles.

I continue. "I am aware the banquet last evening was to entertain Mildred the Malodorous and her mayoralty bid."

Mother wants to chastise me for my description of our

dentist, but cannot at the same time as hiding a smile behind her napkin.

I continue. "But she does not have the best interests in mind for our subjects."

My father glances around the room to ensure we are alone. "Why say you this?"

"I have many times spoken about how our citizens are disadvantaged, and how I believe we are failing in our duty to them. I believe that if Dr. Stevenson becomes mayor, their plight will worsen. She will take the small measure of freedom and joy our subjects now have, and will rule without care for the equal rights for all."

Mother shakes her head. "You are too young and inexperienced to know that, or to govern this kingdom."

"But if I wait until I am older, it will be too late. And how am I to gather experience unless I become involved?" I take pains to erase any tinge of whining in my voice.

Father states, "I do not disagree with The queen. You are young and inexperienced."

I open my mouth to interrupt, but he holds up a hand, stilling my words. "But I remember when I came to this throne." He and my mother exchange fond smiles. "I was not even as old as you are, Viisi." His eyes drift up to the tapestry on the wall behind me. "And I was green and thought the crown would grant me permission to play and hunt to my heart's content." His smile fades. "But I had much to learn, not the least of which was the ways that men will lie to further their way in life. I learned quickly the cruelties that lurk in the hearts of many. I attempted to erase evil when I could and to rule with fairness and compassion. I agree with your mother that you do not yet have the wisdom.

"But you can gain it through experience. And perhaps you are correct, I have lost sight of the hardships of our people." He looked at my mother, then me. "Tell me, if I allow you to do this, what is it that you want? How will you, a mere scrap of a girl with no experience and little knowledge of the world, hope to defeat the campaign of Mildred Stevenson?"

I speak to the king and the queen with an impassioned voice. They are only the first I must convince of my ideals and intentions. If I cannot sway them, how can I hope to gain the confidence of the electorate?

"I will speak for those with no power, and who have so little now. I will speak to them of ancient knowledge that has fallen into disuse.

"I will speak the truth for those who have no voice or control over their destiny. I will show them the need of a dentist who will not rob them of their wisdom. The people of this land need access to a reliable source of herbs and potions. Gerdty needs an assistant, and the resources to increase the size of her garden."

I did not say it, but I know that even Susie needs me. Her song holds the power of magic, long ago hidden by those who feared what they could not understand.

CHAPTER SEVEN:

wherein
wisdom is lacking

PATRICIA L ATCHISON

No amount of washing would remove the smell of pungent smoke from my hair and clothes after I'd been treating Susie's teeth. I needed to go home before the candidates' meet-and-greet with the community, and I was already close to being late.

It wouldn't do to have their favourite candidate for mayor being tardy. I could always say it was an issue at the office, which would carry a note of professionalism and make me look even better in the townspeople's minds.

"Hilary, you stink," I told my assistant as I waved my hand in front of my nose. "Change your clothes before joining me at the meeting. And be on time."

Even if I were going to be late, she'd cover for me. Good thing she knows her role. She was shaping up to be the best assistant I'd ever had. Not that I've had many since starting my practice three years ago. I was sure with more instruction she'd become the right-hand person I needed to see me through this election and into the power I sought to run this town.

I took the path along the outside edge of town, beside a brick wall that was built hundreds of years ago to protect against invading armies. Though the footpath, full of brambles and falling bricks, made it difficult to walk, it would shave off some time from taking the main street home.

It's a good thing I live close to the castle, I thought, stepping over a broken piece of brick and plaster. I jumped back, almost tripping, when a wide saucer-like object landed in front of me, a puff of smoke wafting from the centre. Stepping around it, I nudged it with the toe of my shoe and flipped it over.

It was what I suspected. The dim yellow scale could only be from one creature. I scanned the sky, watching as Susie landed with a thud in the field close to me. She righted herself, shaking a little to loosen the dirt from her side.

I crossed my arms as she approached. "Not only are you losing teeth, but now your scales are falling about like a natural occurrence." I continued, "Dr. Sanchez wishes to banish you from town. Are you going to let that happen or take care of it?"

"The townspeople would never allow it. I've a rapport with them." Susie's eyes narrowed. "I've been a part of this community for centuries."

Her unwavering gaze made me feel as if she were probing my soul, seeing my darkest secrets.

I shook my head at the nonsensical comment.

"Yet they've banished you from the palace common. That's a shame. You could've heard Dr. Sanchez's platform tonight. I assure you. His intentions are real. Are you going to do the deed or not?"

I needed an answer from the geriatric dragon. Dispatching Dr. Sanchez as soon as possible would make things easier for me. No more dreadful campaigning. My lips twitched. I'd be the only candidate left. Mayoralty winner by acclamation.

"Well? I can't cure your haunches," I cackled, noticing

a large scale had disappeared from Susie's hind end and another from her tail, leaving a red scarring mass of flesh. "But I can cure your toothaches. At a reduced rate of course. You must do what I ask of you. One last favour. Nobody would know. You could lure the old doctor out for a little walk to chat with him about your future."

I twisted my head around, ensuring we were alone. "Oh my, what if he suffers a fall? Just make sure it's far away from your cave. Sanchez despises you. I heard it myself. Trust me, if he becomes mayor, he will see you banished from our town." I punched my right fist into the palm of my left hand. "Forever."

The ground shook as Susie lumbered close. She leaned down and snorted against my face.

I choked against the blast of air smelling like rotting flesh, ash, and tooth decay, but I refused to take a step back.

"You lie," she huffed.

Hot sooty air shot between us.

I ignored it and leaned toward her. "Why would I do that? I need your business. Judging by the putrid smell of your breath, we've a lot of work to do on that mouth of yours. What do you say?"

The dragon tried to circle me, but the town wall stopped her tail flick. She shifted, pacing in front of me instead. I waited, sure the loose bolts in the old girl's head were rattling around as she thought about her answer.

She faced me, her fangs barred. "I'm retired. Let me enjoy my future. I don't need your help."

Susie lowered her sooty golden snout inches from my face. I focused on one tiny burnt scale peeling back from the base of her nostril before I turned away to avoid another blast of smoke.

"If Gerdty's not too mad at me, I shall talk to her again and get the healing herbs I need, or I'll pay your price. But I refuse to *dispatch* Dr. Sanchez," she said.

I watched her clench her claws, eyeing the sharp talons embedded in her reptile nubs, remembering the death clutch she had on my neck earlier. The dragon would be of no help. I chewed my lip, figuring out another plan for Dr Sanchez.

"I had to ask," I said as I bopped my knuckles between her nostrils. "Now be a good girl and fly away. I have a campaign to win. Oh, and be sure to book your next appointment. Regular, if not inflated, rates apply. You know how it is."

A whoosh of winged energy sent my hair flying about as Susie flew away. I closed my eyes and ducked, hoping she wouldn't crap or pee on me. The old girl had done that before.

Gritting my teeth while thinking of Susie's response, I strutted to the archway ready to enter the gate to my property. I stopped short when a moan came from a row of bushes not far away. Time was slipping away, and I needed to get to the meeting, but I stopped and listened. The low moan came again. I snuck up to the end of the bushes, thinking if I helped someone in need, it would look good for my campaign. A quick glance around a leafy vine had me clucking my tongue.

"My, my. What have we got going on here?" My eyebrow raised at the scene in front of me, featuring bare arms, shoulders, and calves.

Princess Viisi pulled her mouth away from the local farm boy's lips, her eyes wide. Her cheeks grew crimson faster than I could blink away my disgust.

I recognized, but had never met, the farm boy nestled next to her.

"Hmm," I said, tapping my lips with my index finger. "I'm sure the king would be most interested in this little tryst. What are you thinking, girl? Didn't I just see you last night entertaining the whims of Lord Rodney?"

The farm boy stood up in a flash, tucking his shirt into pants crusted with dust and dirt. He held his hand out to Princess Viisi, helping her up from the squashed foliage.

"It is none of your business, Dr. Stevenson." Viisi stood, her fingers attempting to bring order to her tousled plaits. "Please, be on your way."

I studied the girl as she brushed her skirts down, frowning, and trying to remove a grass stain rimming one side. After the banquet last night, she had been most verbal in siding with those eager to help Susie. She'd expressed disagreement with Sanchez's idea of banishing the dragon and had strong opinions about managing the town after the election. Happening on this secret scene was something I could use against her if she became too mouthy in the future.

I smiled. "I'm on the way to the castle. Your father is hosting the candidates tonight. Shortly, really. I, too, am late. I assume once you tidy up, you will join the affair?"

Viisi's attention shifted toward the horizon, where the sun made its descent over the mountains. The girl gasped, pulled her skirts up, and, with an apologetic glance at the farm boy, dashed through the archway.

I cleared my throat. "What's your name, young man?"

"Jack."

"Jack who?" My eyes narrowed.

"Jack McCready, ma'am."

"You must have work to do. Don't just stand there open-mouthed. Off you go."

"Yes, ma'am."

Too busy thinking about this evening, I almost missed an opportunity. "Wait. Come back."

With a quizzical look, Jack stood before me. "Ma'am?"

"Please, it's Dr. Stevenson, but call me Milly. Do you know who I am?"

"Yes, ma'a...Dr. Stevenson...Milly. You're the dentist." A flush rose on the boy's neck.

I grabbed his chin and pushed my thumb and index finger against his mandible, forcing his mouth open. I stood up on my tiptoes and peered into his mouth.

"Just as I thought."

"Thou wha ma'a... Milly?"

His garbled words shook me from my investigation. He rubbed his jaw when I dropped my hand.

"Have your mother book an appointment right away.

Those wisdom teeth of yours have been giving you pain. Haven't they?" I didn't give Jack the opportunity to respond. "Of course they have. It'll only get worse, you know. Open wide again."

I examined his teeth with a frown of concern, trying to stop the twitch in my fingers. "Yes. Goodness. I must see you within the next day. We'll squeeze you in, but those wisdom teeth must come out. Right away."

"I don't understand," Jack frowned.

"Am I not the dentist here? There's nothing to understand. Off you go. Talk to your mother. I need to take care of that. You don't want it to get worse."

I sniffed and turned on my heel before the boy could question me. Dusk settled across the door to my home. I dashed in, gave my face a scrub, fluffed my hair and changed into a clean frock. In the mirror, a young, vibrant fresh face stared back at me, her steely grey eyes unwavering in determination.

Below the mirror, a vial of powder rested on the dresser. I only had an inch of material, but doing more wisdom tooth extractions would take care of that. Hilary proved her value last month after learning about a discovered legend from her Aunt Rebecca, who worked in the castle. The housekeeper shared it with her niece after reading an old scroll she found in a secret room.

Hilary's excitement was contagious when she explained ancient wisdom tooth extraction with me out of interest for the subject of historical dental practices.

What ignited me was the legend of power which occurred when the wisdom tooth powder is mixed with draughts and consumed. I lifted my eyes to the woman in the mirror.

"We will be more powerful than I ever thought possible."

I grabbed my shawl. Win the election first, I scolded myself.

Lights lit the cobblestones on the way into the castle common area. Torches flickered inside tents set up for each candidate. I passed by Sanchez's tent. He stood inside chatting with five men, their heads bobbing up and down, agreeing with what he spouted.

I'll have to work harder to eliminate him. If Susie won't take care of it, maybe I'll have to take care of them both, I cursed to myself.

I stopped short at the next tent. Inside, looking prim and mature in a gown of royal blue satin, her wimple tight and tidy, stood Princess Viisi. I stared at her, and she smiled coyly in return. Heads turned to face me, and my frown turned up at the edges as I smiled back.

"Ah. Surprising, isn't it?" said a man's voice behind me.

I recognized the king's rich baritone and turned, offering a small curtsey, cocking my head. "What is?"

"Viisi spoke with me this morning. I'm not sure I understand everything she means to do with this town, but if she wins, I'll be lending both an ear to her ideas and issuing my own."

"Wins?" My throat went dry as I tried to swallow back a retort.

"You look shocked, dear Mildred. I realize a sixteen-year-old may not be mature enough to be mayor, but as I stated," he leaned forward, "I will offer my experience as well."

"Your Highness, I..." I almost stuttered, but with the scene I had witnessed earlier playing in my mind, I gathered my confidence and determination. I had come too far in my campaign to let that little twit cross me. "You must be proud of young Princess Viisi, and her political aspirations. May I speak with honesty?"

"But of course. I encourage it."

"Perhaps in private?"

"No. Now." His kind eyes prompted me to speak.

I leaned forward, my cheek almost touching his, and whispered against his ear. The preciseness of my words brought a catch to his throat, but he let me continue without interruption. I rolled my eyes up at the black starry night while embellishing a few extra details.

"Sorry, Your Highness, but I thought it sensible a father should know." I stepped back, bowing my head in respect, which helped me hide the small smile forming on my lips.

I glanced at Viisi. Her bottom lip trembling, her wide eyes locked on mine.

The king shoved past me and grabbed his daughter's elbow.

"I'm sorry. Princess Viisi is needed elsewhere." With a nod, he informed the group of young men clustered in the princess's tent. "You'd be wise to chat with Dr. Stevenson about details of her campaign."

Setting a cheerful smile on my face, I motioned to the tent across from me. "Come, gentlemen."

Their gazes followed the king and princess as they

both disappeared into the castle. With shoulders shrugging, they joined me.

"How unfortunate Princess Viisi took her leave, but let me answer questions you may have about my candidacy." I allowed my smile to reach my eyes and cocked my head toward the group.

"How will you solve our dragon problem?" came a question from a stooped woman with greying temples.

"Ah, Susie. She indeed has caused some issues," I responded.

"Issues! Most of Gerdty's plot of healing herbs is gone. It will take months of growth inside on the windowsill, soaking up the sunlight, to replace what that ancient bird destroyed. Also, poor Samuel was knocked down by one of that dragon's scales falling."

I remembered when it had happened. Before I extracted Gerdty's sister's wisdom teeth, she told me all about how Gerdty's grandson almost lost his head when one of Susie's scales came crashing down. I wondered where one of her other scales ended up. Should've been on top of Sanchez's head.

"I understand the dragon is causing problems. Most of them stem from her poor tooth health and being in such pain. I've started fixing her teeth to help in that matter, but it takes time. It is an enormous undertaking. After she's no longer in pain, I'll ensure she is in a comfortable place up in the hills, where she does not need to come into the village at all, unless invited."

"Hear! Hear!" several people agreed.

"Princess Viisi says you only want to be mayor, so you can take our money for unnecessary dental procedures. She said somethin' about wisdom. I dunno what it all means," said one fellow with indignation, yellowing teeth, and a crooked jaw.

"Oh, my goodness." I shook my head from side to side, feigning surprise at such a thought. "I was unaware the princess is also a dentist?"

Chuckles filled the tent.

"Do you seriously think a girl of sixteen knows how to run a dental practice? Does she know the benefits of a good cleaning? No. I'm afraid she has no experience in such matters. You, sir, could benefit from my services. I will make your smile dazzling. Then afterward, all the girls will line up for a date with you."

The fellow's grin broadened, showing a few dark holes along the ridge of his teeth. "You could do that for me?"

"Yes, and for you all. If I win this election, I'll see to it that everyone gets a free cleaning."

Above the cheering, I murmured, "Along with a wisdom tooth extraction, of course."

CHAPTER EIGHT:

wherein
Marianne the melodious milkmaid
hears murmurings

ISABEL CAVE

It was early morning and the dawn was painting the sky in shimmering shades of gold. I had a lot of cows and farms to visit, and I was still waking up.

Yawning, I pulled my shawl tighter around me. It would warm up once the sun had fully risen, but for now it was chilly, and I was going to have a long day on my own, now that my dad wasn't with me every day.

Don't get me wrong, I was very glad that he had retired from his job as the village's head milkman. He was much happier since he took up wood carving. Plus, he was able to nap and never had to miss a choir practice again.

I was lonely, though. Being the head milkmaid was hard work and not what I hoped to do for the rest of my life.

My true passion was music, and I wanted to collect the folk songs I had grown up listening to. My dream was to share them with the kingdom, perhaps even the rest of the world, and to educate people about the value of traditions. There was so much we could learn about ourselves and our heritage. I sighed. It was just a dream for now. I couldn't leave Dad. He relied on me to continue the family business and care for him as he aged. I had to get on with my job. I could see the first farm appearing through the morning mist, where Molly the Jersey cow was waiting for me to relieve her of her milk.

I kicked at a few loose stones as I followed the path near the castle. It was nearly lunchtime, when I would get a break. My stomach growled as I thought about a sandwich from the pub. Maybe one day I could sing at the pub and make a bit of extra money that way. Imagine if I could sing for the king and queen… *stop right there*, I told myself firmly. *Your job is milking and delivering that milk.*

I jumped as a great gust of wind nearly swept me off

my feet.

It was Susie the dragon, and she did not look happy! Her stinky breath was normal, but the sulfurous smoke that was puffing from her snout wasn't. Whew!

My eyes were watering from the combined smells. What had happened to upset her? I watched to make sure she was flying away before I dusted myself off, straightening my apron, and patting my chestnut hair back beneath my straw bonnet. This wasn't my favourite pathway as it led past the home of the horrid dentist, Mildred the Merciless. She was always rude to me and claimed that milk was bad for teeth—the nerve! Everyone knew that milk was full of calcium, which makes teeth stronger.

I clutched my milk pail as I heard a loud squeal, followed by a moan coming from behind a wall. I didn't expect to hear *those* sounds near Miserable Mildred's house! I shuddered when I heard Mildred's voice. Her nasally tones never failed to set my teeth on edge. Ducking down, I hid behind some trees, peering through the branches.

"My, my. What have we got going on here?" Mildred sneered at a young, rather rumpled couple emerging from a clump of bushes.

I managed not to gasp as I realized it was Princess Viisi! Goodness, what was she doing, and who was she doing it with? She had leaves in her hair and she was rubbing at a grass stain on her skirt.

The princess looked down her nose at Mildred, informing her that it was none of her business, before running off toward the castle.

I recognized the young man with her was Jack McCready from one of the farms near town. I sometimes saw him on my milk rounds, and we had gone to the village school together. He had been a bully when we were children, making fun of those of us who liked reading instead of sports, so I was very surprised that the last time I saw him, he was in a barn reading a book. When I called out a good morning, he looked horrified and stuffed the book into the straw behind him. Hmm. Funny to have seen him twice in such unusual places.

Malevolent Mildred demanded to know his name before examining his teeth.

"Just as I thought, book an appointment right away. Those wisdom teeth of yours have been giving you pain, haven't they? Of course they have."

I didn't hear the rest of what she said as she was shoving her face into Jack's mouth, but I heard her tell him, "...Those wisdom teeth must come out. We'll fit you in."

Yuck! The thought of having teeth pulled made me feel queasy.

Mildred the Maleficent headed into her house, so I left quickly. I didn't want her spotting me and threatening *my* teeth!

I checked the village clock. I was late. Oh dear, I had one more farm left to visit and Betsy the cow who lived there was older, grumpy, and liked to kick.

"Hello there, Marianne!"

Mrs. Field, the farmer's wife, waved as I walked through the gate.

"I'll have tea for you when you're finished with Betsy."

I smiled, waving back. Mrs. Field loved to gossip over a pot of tea.

Betsy behaved today, so it wasn't long until I was sitting at the big oak table in the kitchen.

"Did you hear about Gerdty's garden? That

wretched dragon flattened most of it!"

Mrs. Field tutted as she poured more tea from a red teapot.

"I did hear something about it. I thought it was an accident?"

"Well, dearie, accident or not, we are all in a pickle. Where are all our tinctures, potions, and such going to come from? My Bill's rheumatism has been something awful lately. He needs his ointment from Gerdty!"

"I don't know, but I'm sure that once we have a new mayor it will get sorted out."

"Hmm. Not if it's that Mildred Mandible! Only out for herself is what I hear, and I heard tell that she is stealing teeth. Too many young 'uns have been going to her and coming back with fewer teeth, when all they went for was a cleaning!"

She pursed her lips. "It's fishy if you ask me. Who goes around stealing teeth?"

I pondered what the farmer's wife had told me as I walked home.

What was Mildred the Misery up to? Hadn't she just told Jack that *his* wisdom teeth had to go, after a very quick look in his mouth? Why did she want so many wisdom teeth?

Poor Susie. It seemed to me that lots more people were complaining about her these days. She was an old dragon. She was probably very lonely. I felt sorry for her. She had to be in a lot of pain, with her remaining scales falling off and rotting teeth.

I liked Susie and I wasn't scared of her. I had grown up hearing my granny telling me stories about dragons.

"Common folk don't remember that dragons have magic. It must have been something, watching them fly together, hearing their songs. They brought so much joy. Mind, you didn't want to get on their bad side. They could bring the rainclouds in a hurry!"

She would chuckle as she sat with me, sharing tea and toast, telling her tales.

Granny had grown up in the Welsh Valleys, where music was treasured. My father had inherited her love of music, and sang in a tenor choir. He had a magnificent voice.

"I swear you were born singing, Marianne, love! Just like your dad, you are."

Granny would squeeze my cheeks before giving me

a big kiss, her bright blue eyes twinkling as I sat at her feet, spellbound while she told me about faeries, dragons, witches, and long-forgotten lore.

"Don't forget to listen to the songs around you. A long time ago, folk didn't write things down. Instead, they sang songs to teach their children, to share the secrets and wisdom of the ancestors."

She would sing old folk songs to me, and I loved them, even if I was too young to understand what they meant.

"Nature is full of magic, my love. The forests, the hills and mountains, but greatest of all, the dragons. They would sing and marvellous things would happen. Some folk say it is all rubbish, but I know in my bones that Dragon Song is not lost forever. Mark my words, Marianne. One day the world will hear dragons sing again."

I had never forgotten and listened as she had told me to, until one day while out in the meadows, I heard the most beautiful song. I looked all over but couldn't see who was singing. It was so lovely, it brought tears to my eyes, and I was heartbroken not to be able to find the owner of that lovely voice.

It was at that moment I understood what my purpose was. I was meant to learn songs like that, to share them with the world! I would become a travelling bard and leave the life of a milkmaid far behind. It was my destiny!

The next morning I was up later than the day before.

"You're a bit late for your rounds, love." My dad called from the kitchen as I came down for breakfast.

"It's all right, Dad, I have the day off. Sally asked for a bit of work as her little boy needs a new pair of shoes."

Sally was a young mother from the village who helped out with the milking.

"Ahh, children grow so fast," Dad chuckled, tapping his pipe on the table.

"I'm going down to the village. It's Market Day. Anything you want me to pick up?'

Now Dad was retired, he was happiest at home and avoided Zos on Market Days. He said all those people were too much for him, as they were loud and seemed to do nothing but shout and complain about everything.

"Yes, love. Could you see if Tom Oakley has any walnut wood in? I want to start a new figure, a dragon."

He lit his pipe.

"I'm not sure why a dragon, but something is telling me to make one."

I added walnut wood to my list; it wasn't long. I mostly went to Market to chat and meet friends. Too much shopping wasn't a good idea, as I had to carry home whatever I bought.

The village seemed busier than usual and I had to push my way through the crowds to get to Tom's stall.

"Mornin', Miss Marianne. How are you, and how is your dad?"

"Good morning to you, Tom. We are both well, thank you. Dad was hoping you might have some walnut wood. He wants to carve a dragon."

Tom rubbed his grey beard.

"I think I might have some. Speaking of dragons, I've been having trouble getting some of my orders filled, what with people being anxious about that Susie and her crashing around. Not to mention, some of the woodsmen have been hearing strange things in the forest, they tell me. Makes them reluctant to go too far in. All very odd, and doesn't do us honest working souls any good."

"I am sorry to hear that, Tom. Whatever you have,

Dad will be grateful for."

I paid the still grumbling merchant, who promised to have the wood set aside for me when I was ready to head home.

As I wandered around the marketplace, I listened to the different conversations.

Many people were complaining about the outgoing mayor, how he had made promises to sort out this or that problem, but had never done anything. There were differing opinions about who should be the next mayor. However, what I found unsettling was that underneath the chatter, I would hear voices whispering Mildred's name, murmuring things like, "Progressive ideas" or "Decisive action."

I frowned as I tried to see who was doing the whispering. I had no idea who these people were. I didn't recognise their voices, but I was certain of one thing. They did not live here in Zos.

I headed for the pub, needing a drink and time to sit out of the sun. Inside, it was cool and I had to wait for a moment as my eyes adjusted to the lower light. Going to the bar, I greeted Sam, the landlord.

"Hello, Sam. Can I get half a pint of cider?"

As we chatted, I looked around to see who was in.

In a corner sat a downcast Jack McCready. He might have teased me when I was younger, but I believed in giving folks second chances, that they could change and become better people. I took my half pint and sat down at Jack's table.

"Jack, you don't look yourself. Are you all right?"'

He glared at me.

"Nothing you can do. What do you care, anyway?"

"Why shouldn't I care? I don't like to see anybody unhappy or in trouble. We weren't always friends, but I hear talk when I'm on my rounds. People have only good things to say about you, that you work hard and always help your neighbours out."

Jack dropped his head into his hands.

"Marianne, I'm sorry for snapping. You wouldn't believe the mess I've made of things. Nobody knows that me and the princess, we're together. We've kept it secret because, I mean, a farm hand and a princess?"

He paused to rub his face.

"It's like she and I have known each other forever. We talk and talk, and she's given me books about political ideas. We both want to change things around here, make Zos better and happier, together. Viisi wants to be the next mayor, and I know she would be fantastic!"

Now I understood why he looked so guilty when I caught him reading! The king didn't encourage what he called radical ideas.

"The problem is, we weren't careful enough and Mildred the Dentist caught us having a bit of a cuddle. It's my fault, as I asked Viisi to meet me yesterday. We weren't as cautious as we usually are. Mildred has gone and told the king! Can I tell you something important, secret?"

I nodded, and he looked around furtively. Seeing no one near us, he lowered his voice before continuing.

"That Mildred is dangerous. Viisi found a scroll and it says you can gain powers from wisdom teeth. The best ones come from the young. You take them from the gums, then straight away grind them into a powder that you drink every night. It's supposed to make whoever drinks it powerful.

"Mildred's been collecting teeth! All the children who see her come back with their wisdom teeth gone! When she found me and Viisi, she told me my teeth need to go. I had to pretend to look like I didn't know what she was on about. She told the king so he will stop Viisi running for Mayor because Mildred wants the job! Viisi is Mildred's only real competition. She's going to take over the town and then who knows where she'll stop?"

I was horrified. Mildred was awful, but I didn't realise how bad she was. And it got worse.

"Marianne, Mildred wants to kill Susie! The dragon is clumsy, we all know that, and she has caused trouble, but she doesn't deserve to die. What has Susie ever done to Mildred?"

"I don't know, Jack. I do remember my granny said that dragons have magic that most of us have forgotten."

I sipped my cider, thinking hard.

"Perhaps Susie is the key to stopping Mildred. We need to find out if she is, and if so, how. Do you think you can get a message to Princess Viisi, and let her know what we suspect? She might be able to find some answers in the castle library."

Jack nodded, looking more cheerful.

"Yes, I know one of the kitchen maids and she will pass a note on for me."

He smiled and took my hand.

"Thank you, Marianne. If you hadn't come and

talked to me, I don't know what I would have done. You will always have friends in me and Viisi. If you ever need our help, you only have to ask."

After finishing our drinks we agreed to let each other know if we discovered anything. It was a relief to know that the princess was involved. She was in trouble with her father, but she was still in a better position than most to help stop Malevolent Mildred and save Susie.

I collected the wood for Dad and set off for home. I was tired, upset, and worried. Mildred had to be stopped, but I had no idea what to do. I'd keep listening and pass on whatever I could to Jack and the princess, of course, but would that be enough? I continued up the track home, walking around the base of a hill before passing the edge of Zos Forest. It was an ancient forest, a wild wood some called it, and villagers had many stories about what lurked deep within it. As children we were warned about the wolves, bears, and darker creatures that lived amongst its giant trees. Usually, I would hear birds calling to each other and bees buzzing amongst the flowers. Today, however, I heard what sounded like humming. Humming? I stopped, turning around, trying to tell where it was coming from. The tune sounded like that song I had heard in the meadow, the one I had been hoping to hear again. Could I finally find the singer? I dropped the wood I was carrying, following the enchanting melody into the forest.

It was darker amongst the trees, their huge trunks soaring to where a dense canopy of leaves spread. Spots of sunlight dappled the ground as I pushed through bushes and walked between saplings. The humming got louder, and I saw light up ahead.

Before me was an otherworldly glade, and in the middle of it was Susie, her scales glowing in the sunshine. Susie was humming. I recognised her voice—she was the singer I had been searching for! As I looked around in wonder, I saw butterflies and dragonflies flitting around her. I squinted, trying to see what else was there. Was I seeing faeries? Surely not. They were just stories, weren't they? Wings glinting with rainbow colours, ribbons and flowers in their hair, tiny creatures that could only be faeries danced through the air around Susie. I caught my breath, awestruck. Granny was right, dragons *were* magic, and that could mean Dragonsong was real!

CHAPTER NINE:

wherein
the wind wistfully watches

KELLY KOMM

Oh, **We yearn for The Song!** The notes of music as they dance through Me and You; each note lit from within by ancient, joyous fury. Ancient, furious joy! Ancient, riotous strength. Ancient power and flight, oh! What beautiful dances we had, The Song and I, The Song and You. The Song and We! The dance, the dance, the dance was everything...

Until It was gone.

I feel these prattling attempts at song... You feel those stuttering vibrations of song... We feel pathetic quivers of song... But none are The Song! That Song! None lift Us, and push You, and pull Me, and thread through, and squeeze Us, and fill Us the way The Song did. The Song of Triumph, The Song of Euphoria, The Song of Blood! Where have the ancient creatures all gone? Do You remember when We were filled with The Song? Like leaves on a tree in the full bloom of summer, I was littered with the giant beings. They brought The Song, and We danced! You carried them and their bliss, and I lifted them and their rage, and We danced and dove through day and night, through time and age, again and again.

Come, come see. I feel these prattling attempts at song... You feel those stuttering vibrations of song... We feel pathetic quivers of song... But none are The Song! That Song! None lift Us, and push You, and pull Me, and thread through, and squeeze Us, and fill Us the way The Song did. The Song of Triumph, The Song of Euphoria, The Song of Blood!

We remember when many filled Us with their notes and the dance was nearly constant. We lifted them and they sang, and You felt their elation as though I were running across stones. We lifted them and they sang, and I felt their rage like a thunderous frenzy of rain spitting through You. We lifted them and they sang, and You felt their happiness like a warm blanket of fresh snow dusting across Me.

Sometimes, after several of them had conquered a stronghold, they would gorge and sleep and steal, but THEN! Then, they would climb upwards and through Us and they would finally, finally, finally sing! The Song of Fury would dance with You, the Song of Ruin would dance with Me. Oh, the sound and shape and texture of The Song was unlike any other. And after they had finished with their pillage, We would go through their desolation and spread what flame You could find, and what disease I could find, and whatever else We could grab and fling about in Our joy of having danced with The Song. That ancient, beautiful Song.

And sometimes, after mating or birthing, they would take to Our realm and sing with such overwhelming elation, You couldn't even match the dance! Such pleasure in the ferocity of their delight! The joy was such that We could only lift and spin as it passed through, as though such happiness couldn't be contained or controlled or corrupted. Oh, the feel of that joy! The Song of Love would sweep Your currents, the song of Healing would sweep My currents. The beauty, the majesty of The Song...

And to caress the new being that would one day be among Us, that would one day carry on The Song...

Oh, of course We dance in other ways. Scooping up leaves and twigs and carrying them, twirling them, spinning them, dropping them. You lift petals and seeds, and I push snowflakes and sleet. Moving around creatures, rustling fur and feather. Running along cresting waves, and hills of clover, and rocks and pebbles and dirt... but... None move Us to dance like The Song did. Even the tiniest beings that flit among Us—exploring Our world like their beastly brethren. Flying through Us is like the tiniest hair on water—their wee Song is practically silent compared to the True Song. How are We to dance with such small notes, such miniscule rage, such infinitesimal joy, ah, it is not The Song... That song... And there are less and less of those who sang The Song, less dancing with The Song. With every passing night and day, every passing season and year, every decade and century. Before, they would fill our realm with The Song, and now You wait, and I wait, and We wait... The time passes and the creatures change and the land changes and still We are here, the same as I ever was, the constant that You've always been.

We are a second home for them. You've heard them, I've heard them, We've heard them. They tell the world it's so through The Song. They live as naturally with Us—floating among the stars or sunbeams—as they do among the rocks and hills.

Some of these new, earthbound creatures have tried The Song.

Most embarrass You with their ignorance, and anger Me with the attempt. Even Our great winged brethren become insulted at these attempts. Often I will sense this, and encourage great storm clouds in their defence. You will blow the spray of rain, and I will push the darkening clouds, and We will carry their discontent far and wide.

But there are the rare few who almost capture it, despite being sadly earthbound. Over the passage of time, We've caught snippets of true Song here. You've caught tunes on an errant current there. I've searched for The Song in these and it's so close, so close, oh! You move through and tickle, for We feel an ancient one - one who sang The Song, for whom the Song lived through. She is old, but We are older, You are older, I am older. The Song, she must give Us the Song! We must dance! Dance with fury, dance with joy! How is this timeless creature so diminished, so unwell? She must rise, rise, RISE! Fly with Us, sister of the Song! Dance with Me, Titan of time!

But halt! Heed! An earthbound, You hear it? This wee being there, We listen! There is a true sound here—a joyful healing! A genuine connection! And from such a tiny one! The dance, the dance, the dance is everything! Ah, the notes are too small, too close to the ground; We need her up, up, up with Us... You need her braiding through Me, I need her folding through You. Up, up, up, little flightless creature, it cannot be The Song without the reckless joy of fear, or the thrilling terror of affirmation. Join Us!

Moving upside, another song weaves below now – they dance stiffly, this group of earthbound creatures – they practically march! They sing too harshly; their shouts and shrieks lack the true joy of The Song. None are free of the burden of the ground. How could any of them truly feel the wonder of The Song without being free of the pull of their ground, their anchor, their magnet? Is this what The Song has become? This angry nattering is more akin to irritating birdsong than a true Song.

Some creatures wield pieces of Our elemental sisters at the ends of branches, and the burning excites Us. It reminds Me of the furious flames that would sometimes accompany The Song. Oh, The Song! The flames remind You of the twinning spiral of dance We have had with the flame's Song. Ah, but these flames are bound down, and The Song is up here and I yearn for it!

You are angered by their graceless march, and I am angered by their tuneless chants. We blast and blow between these inconsequential creatures. You snuff their meagre flames, nearly knocking the sticks from them. I dart in and out of their tiny maws, turning their shouts to gasps and chirps. This playful mischief brings Us some joy, but We are bored. You still, and I quiet. This mournful dance is not the same. The beings that once moved in Our realm could emit visceral passion! These crawling creatures cannot give us the same thrill...

Swooping here, I have found one who spews fury, but there is no flame in her, no genuine song. She yammers with ferocity and there is potential in her hate, but she finds no real joy in this, do You feel it? Nor do We feel elation or love. No, no, no! This tiny human is wrong. Her incitement lacks courage, it lacks, it lacks! And she is locked to the land. How could she truly Sing? Hers is not a Song of Flame, a Song of Blood, a Song of Joy, even though she thinks it is. We push her a little, stealing her feeble song, twisting her clothes and pulling her hair. Her chitters of lies and anger die a bit and We scoop it up to dance and twirl. Moving between these beings, I can so easily swipe and roll, and You can twirl and slip, and We feel the ebb of their fury as their dull march slows and their shouts become muffled whimpers. This is no faithful Song, though the snippets of angst are charming.

CHAPTER TEN:

wherein
Princess Viisi
makes a move

MAFALDA ROSE

Had the knowledge of Mildred's corruption reached me sooner, I'd have wrung the neck of that horrid dentist the moment the chance presented itself!

I had long held out hope that the good people of this village were above any degree of senseless mob violence, though, of course, such dismal times had proved me wrong. Should you grant a crowd, desperate for *any* solution to their woes, an unyielding figure to lead them, then the flock would follow that shepherd most promptly, no matter how much of their wisdom she pockets, no matter how black hearted she may be. I know all too well that, in all likelihood, she was far from alone in her culpability. Those mindless drones of hers contributed to this, I was sure. Trouble rarely travels alone, after all.

Which had led me here, to the dragon's mountain, decorum thrown to the wind. I knew the truth, and now, as princess, it was my duty to show the villagers the truth, before they brought about the downfall of the entire town. The youngest daughter I might be, perhaps nothing more than another spoiled king's daughter in the eyes of the common folk. Doing this would not only right the wrongs that have been committed, but would also finally let me make the changes necessary for our future. Though, that was for later. My resolve, for the moment, must be on the present crisis.

Easier said than done, however.

Must they be so eager to race themselves to their own ruin?! Running in this suffocating dress and shying away from the trail left me alone, clamouring with my thoughts and dueling with my feet as each rise of the ground grew more difficult. Despite the odds, I knew well that Susie and the very fabric of this town depended on my intervention. I must make it. I must not falter. I *could not* falter.

I could see the mass still a distance away, and in spite of the increasing ache in my legs and my head, I continued to give chase, dashing with more fervour than I thought possible. Doubtlessly, this task would have been far less gruelling had I been able to make use of the weathered road, though that ran the risk of me being spotted by that screeching cat of a fraud, and surely, I'd serve as the dragon's psychopomp as we both departed into the afterlife.

My words are my sword, I nodded to myself, though my dress made for an ill-equipped shield against the brambles and rocks.

Wood crunching beneath my battered heels, even at one point, almost tricked me into believing I had worn out my spindly legs enough that *they* were the source of that snapping in my haste. Yet, even *if* I had broken them, not even all the flogging on this earth, nor the blades of a hundred knives, would stop me now. I had settled into a good pace now, finding what ached the least while still maintaining a most effective speed. I'd let neither that dentist nor difficult paths deter me!

"If *this* does not build up muscle," I laughed to myself, dryly, "then I am truly a lost cause!"

Humour was the natural way to keep my mind on a confident, hopeful streak. If I gave myself too much of a pause, too much silence to think, a crushingly depressive spiral would manifest itself, rising from the ashes of positivity.

I had almost not even noticed that the crowd's progress had frozen nearly to a stand still. Immediately, my mind began to race again, almost beyond my control. Why had they stopped? We were not yet near the top of the mountain! Perhaps... perhaps they had taken a rest? If that was the case, then it seemed as though my moment had arrived sooner than anticipated! *What luck!*

That voice! No! No, no, no! Susie, what in blazes are you doing? Now you fly to an early grave as well?! What foolishness! Especially from one so old! Has some madness taken everyone?!

I was not normally one to lose my temper so readily, but personally, I believed this situation called for it. In the face of such stress, I was at least able to exercise some modicum of restraint, only crying out internally, rather than giving such thoughts a voice.

Though it pained me, knowing that my time to decide *what* exactly I would say, or even *when* I should intervene was now far, *far* shorter than I needed, I had to stay in the forest's shadows for the time being to see why Susie, a being of such high intellect, would now seemingly and suddenly be throwing her life to the wind, as if it meant nothing. It would also grant me the opportunity to see if, unlikely as it may be, the villager might have a change of heart without my help. One could hold out that hope, though I was not holding my breath on that chance at present.

The earth stood still. The forest watched with nary a breeze to fill in the screaming silence. All nature understood the gravity, yet the crowd did not. I cringed with each step I took, convinced that every movement agonizing in this void, pair after pair of vindictive eyes fell upon me, holding me down.

"The time has come to rid this village of our *problem*, dragon," To the surprise of no one, Milly was the first to speak, evidently already elevating herself as the village's spokeswoman, *self*-appointed, spokeswoman.

Susie could only snort. "Your *problem*."

A heavy sigh followed, exasperated and exhausted by

the world around. The hatred and harsh words never truly lost their sting, no matter how many years of bearing them rolled by.

Making a lichen-covered stone my shelter, I could see those eyes of hers, yellow, serpentine, unforgettable, tracing over the crowd, keeping every face of this maddening mindlessness in her memory.

"Why should that surprise you, Susie? You truly did not believe you'd not answer for your crimes?" *Ah, so the devoted little duckling did quack. Weren't good minions supposed to be silent?*

"Since you went to the trouble of rallying this mob, dear dentist, please do enlighten me of what I am so guilty of." I had to stifle a giggle, hearing her pay the squawking parrot that was Hilary no mind. I was grateful that Susie was maintaining a seemingly calm mind; though I supposed confidence comes natural to a dragon.

"Since, the last *I* had heard, it was *Sanchez* who wished for me to be rid of me, and now, it is *you*. One has to wonder why."

For a power play! I so wished to scream. Being so close and yet unable to do anything made me wish I could tear my hair right out! Lying low, waiting for that moment I could only *hope* would arrive; when that foolhardy would-be usurper would incriminate herself. All her lies would come crashing down upon her, and all would be well again.

Or at least, so I could hope. There was the possibility that she'd craft a lie so complete that none would listen to reason at all. These deceived souls would drink every drop of her poisoned words.

"Very well, I'll endeavour to enlighten you. Though, perhaps, for one so old, might I speak a smidge louder? Wouldn't want those aged ears to miss any details, after all." Her words put the venom of vipers to shame; why, apothecaries and witches alike would pay an arm and a leg for a vial of it.

Susie gave no response to such an obvious, low-brow jab, likely having heard every age-related jest there was and then some.

"The first would be arson, with those absurdly explosive sneezes of yours. Next would be the thoughtless and constant destruction of property. Gerdty's field, William's farmhouse, and I'm certain-" She turned now to face the flock.

"Others could add on?" The paragon egged on the

mob, stoking their fire with each little raise of her voice.

"Without Gerdty's herbs, everyone's going to get sick again!" One whinging squeak sprang up, and several encouraged cheers followed.

"She blocks out the sun with her wings!"

"My crops keep failing, and *she's* the cause of it!"

More cheers, to my horror.

They cannot actually believe that, can they?! Your harvests fail because you neglect to water the produce!

Just how far gone were these wayward villagers? Had I even the ability to convince them, when they had already set their minds?

But I must. A good leader—a *strong* leader—does not falter, or lose heart, even in the face of insurmountable uncertainty and doubt. This could change, and it *would* change. If they were able to fall so far down, then, surely, they could fly just as far back up. They'd simply need a push first.

"As you can see, we really could be here all day, speaking our grievances," The dentist's voice came again, a hush yet firm tone soothing the crowd back into an uneasy silence.

"But I sincerely doubt any one of us wishes to stay any

longer than need be. You did get all that, didn't you, *dear Susie?*" She spoke as one would to a particularly disobedient child, infantilization to hide the malice she spun in her delicately woven words.

The dragon's eyes burned into the crowd's. Though the immeasurable weight of her time on this earth weighed heavily, no number of years lived could ever disguise such contempt, along with such dejection. The flow of time could be kind to many and so cruel to others. Perhaps in a different time, a different place, she'd not face such bigotry.

My heart ached, though I did not face any semblance of her misfortune. It didn't take a dragon to feel another dragon's emotions, even in spite of how hard they may be to read.

I crept ever so gently closer, steeling myself for any hint of violence.

This crowd seemed to be for a bloodbath. My moment would arrive soon.

But, please, oh, please, let that not come until this devil in unfortunate shoes throws herself the wrong bone. One lie, one little lie, that's all I need.

Whatever force was watching over could certainly

hear my plea, could they not? I wasn't normally one to wish for such things from beings I could not see, but, if there were ever more an appropriate time than now, I'd quite like to see it.

"It appears that getting a response from you is impossible. Though, I do suppose that will make this whole ordeal a great deal shorter." The dentist smirked.

"You seem to think you have the upper hand here. You all stay rooted to the ground when I can *soar*. Touch me, and I promise," the ancient dragon growled, heavy steps shaking the earth as she drew near. "Every last one of you will regret ever stepping foot on this mountain."

Milly stepped back, the fear flashing on her face for only a moment.

Susie noticed too, and puffs of smoke rose from her nostrils.

"I see," said Milly. She seemed to waver.

My brows furrowed in confusion. That couldn't be. Not her, of all people.

"I see your true feelings toward us now," Milly said. "We're little more than ants to you, are we not?"

There it was. Nothing but thinly veiled acting. *Why even bother with the veil in the first place?*

"No need to answer. We may be ants, mere candles compared to a dragon's star, but how does one dragon fare against us all?" w

The crowd grew more incensed, red-faced and frothing.

My fingers gripped the rock until they began to burn with pain. This wasn't how things were supposed to be. *Not yet, not yet.*

"Burn us all, and the entire kingdom will hunt for you. They'll never stop, not until you've breathed your last." The endodontist backed into the sea of cloth and dirt.

"Let us spare an old soul such torment," I shouted. My feet flew before my mind could even command them, the speed of a mare riding into its final battle, a most certain demise.

Heads blurred, the noise overwhelming in its sheer force. The charge had begun, scrambling and clawing at a chance to let loose all fury.

The world slowed around me, the trees melting into each other, golden scales going in and out of view. Something struck me. Something that reeled, pulled back, *panicked.* A *slam* into a most peculiar surface dragged me out from the mob's grasp.

Bumpy. How curious. What had I struck? Where was the face I would see before being trampled into a broken mess?

"That's the princess!" came a shocked whisper.

My vision cleared.

The mob had stopped. They stared at me, murmuring, uncertainty on so many unwashed faces.

Had I stopped them? Or merely stunned them?

A lone, rumbling word vibrated throughout my entire body, sending my heart racing out of my chest.

"Viisi?" Susie's voice, no mistaking that. But, when had she grown so close?

I understood then that I was sitting among dragon scales. I had made her arm into a cushion.

I couldn't help but look up at the dropped jaws and gawking faces all around me. Were the situation not so dire, I might've even found the whole scene comical.

"What is the meaning of this? Why have you all stopped?!" Milly burst through the sea of bodies, cheeks carmine in rage.

The red flushed away from her cheeks the moment she caught sight of me, and a frustrated huff flowed through her nose.

"What do we have here? The princess, come to grace us with her presence?" She grimaced, snarling through clenched teeth.

I rose as gracefully as I could and dusted the dirt from my clothes. I would be lying to myself if I didn't feel rather intimidated, being the only person standing between this crowd and Susie, but fear wouldn't achieve anything now.

A sigh for composure, a slow blink to adjust my vision, and I knew I was ready. "I am here to put a stop to this," I stated, firmly.

"A stop to this? Our *righteous* anger?" The dentist crossed her arms.

"Righteous? You lie to all these people, and you have the gall to claim *any* of this is *righteous?*" I couldn't help my voice raising, incredulous at this rampant hypocrisy.

Her glare deepened, perhaps in shock of my defiance of the public opinion.

Whispers and whines flew around, confused glances exchanged amongst the commoners. Many eyes turned to the woman who had rallied and emboldened them.

"Bold of you to claim that *I* have spoken anything but the truth, your *highness*." *A response for everything, just as predicted.* "I do suppose a royal stamping out any chance is common practice, is it not?"

Tyrants dotted the history of the world, coming and going in cycles, brutalizing the peasantry as they saw fit; none of that I could deny. But that exactly is what I sought to change! Where else would change start, other than from within?

Before I could get a retort together, the "good" dentist continued, "This town has no need for either of you. I had considered letting you remain. But you just had to involve yourself in my business."

Word by word, she drew closer to me.

"I will, at the very least, give you credit for managing to scale this mountain without anyone here spotting you. Brave *and* impressive- if not endlessly irritating." Milly now stood directly in front of me, and I felt her breath on my face as she leaned in close. "If you must be another causality, so be it. This town will change under the people. They stand behind me, princess. They would fight for me, *with their teeth* if need be."

Teeth. Oh, but, that was just it, wasn't it? *Teeth. Wisdom teeth.* My mind's waterwheel began to breathe life into its own tale, its own speech. Such an innocuous comment of aspiration, yet such a blunder.

It was *my* turn.

"And when you mean teeth, which do you mean, Dr. Stevenson? Do you mean your own?" I stood taller now, a scarlet princess beside a golden dragon. "It was a good plan, dear doctor. Keep the population foolish and pliable with the wisdom teeth you *pocket*, and then you'll have an entire legion for your dental *congregation.*"

Milly paled. "Now, now..."

"*No.* If you're so sure of your innocence, Milly, then why don't you show each of your patients their records? Or, better yet, explain the missing teeth they can surely *feel?* Or was it all *standard procedure?*" I gave her no chance to spew more deceit. Her time on the soapbox was over for *good*.

"That- that's ridiculous! Complete nonsense! What have I to gain from such a plan?!" She backed herself into a corner now, the telltale glimmer of sweat dotting her forehead.

"*What have you to gain?* You mean, apart from *everything?* You stand a good chance at becoming *mayor,* Mildred. At least, you *stood* a good chance," I shot back.

Eyes narrowed and turned, blues, browns and greens boiling with rage, but not for Susie nor me. For Mildred.

Lies snowball, and once they begin to roll, they have but only one fate, to go round and round until they crash into a thousand flakes.

Her face looked as though she had swallowed a foul-smelling beetle. Disgust and fear carved into her furrowed features. She could feel the sting of ire in her core, I was certain of it.

Tenaciously grasping at straws, the disgraced dentist bit her lips "Hilary...?" Her voice wobbled, not a hint of confidence left.

"Hilary is gone. Your complete coward of an assistant bolted. Look, you can see her outline melding into the endless horizon."

Milly glared at me, though *nothing* she did now mattered to me.

"Feel free to join her," I said. It was less a suggestion than an order, a *royal* command.

It didn't take Milly very long to get the hint, and soon, dust kicked up as her shoes scrambled across the dirt.

Where she went now, I truly didn't care. Barricading herself in the dental office, or a more likely option: fleeing to another town under a false name, perhaps to cause some new disaster. After all, it would be hard to seal herself away in the clinic with an angry crowd hot on her trail.

Maybe it was the relief of the ordeal at last being over, or the massive weight that had freed itself from my chest, but a giggle slipped out of my throat. Childish it might be, it just felt so... nice. Calming. Grateful that it was finished.

Susie must think me an insufferable brat, giggling at a time like this. I pursed my lips sheepishly.

"How long has it been since a human has stood by my side..?" Susie's wistful tone made me jump.

I turned to see her kind gaze on me. It was comforting,

"I imagine a very long time?" I suggested respectfully.

"Longer than you can fathom, young princess."

A comfortable silence settled in between the two of us as we watched the villagers disappear one by one.

We were two souls with stories to share, even if one's book was significantly thicker than the other's.

We would share these tales for those who came after, so that they never be forgotten.

CHAPTER ELEVEN:

wherein
Roland the Butcher
rises to the defense

ROBERT PROUDFOOT

I am Roland. I was village butcher for fifty years, until I sold my shop and retired with Gerdty upon our farm among our family. But that damn dragon did so much damage to Gerdty's livelihood, I became a travelling butcher.

Gerdty always had news when I returned.

One hot summer day, she was re-tilling her garden plot behind our team of mules when a girl greeted her from the road.

This stranger, although her clothes looked expensive, was barefoot.

"Please, Gerdty, I suffer a terrible toothache," the girl begged.

Gerdty limped toward the visitor. Although the girl's large golden eyes were brilliant, when she smiled her thanks, the girl's jagged teeth were brown and her breath was foul.

"If you sit on my porch, we can discuss your malady."

"Thank you," the girl whimpered as she wearily plunked into a wicker chair.

Gerdty brought her some water, which the girl drank in one tip of the cup.

"I already sought dentistry from Doctors Sanchez and Stevenson in our village," she said. "Those bandits gathered a mob last night and tried to kill me."

"Surely not!" Gerdty gasped.

The girl's earnest eyes blinked. "I escaped. I have walked so far today, my body aches. as well as my teeth."

"Who are you?" Gerdty asked. "Do you have family in the village? Your eyes look familiar, but I don't know your face."

The girl's eyes twinkled. "Believe it or not, I am Susie the dragon."

Gerdty's brows furrowed in confusion.

The girl, or rather dragon in human form, went on. "I'm a crotchety old creature with decaying teeth and poor eyesight, but I am magical as well as wise and powerful. Will you help me?"

"Why should I help you? Our grandson Samuel was nearly hit... almost died... when one of your scales fell from the sky! You ruined my garden. Last time, when I shooed you out with a broom, you kept rooting around, chewing and wrecking my plants. I told you then never to return. You are not welcome here. Pretty disguises do not change my mind."

"I just want to get a closer look at your medicinal herbs. The blue oats; purple-flowered knitbone; and white-flowered chamomile could relieve my pain and swelling. I recognized garden heliotrope, which could treat my bungled nerves, and veronica, which could remedy my cough. Fresh dragon's bane and sassafras could assuage my constant headaches. I apologize for damaging your garden, but I'm one sick old gal!"

Gerdty snorted. "Our leaders' attempted sacrifice of a pure farm boy, but you spat Alexander out!"

"The mob failed to realize that human flesh is tasteless and far too stringy. I prefer a sheep or a cow."

"Really?"

"Really. Princess Viisi told me about you. She has a thirst for knowledge. She wants to understand the books in her father's great library."

"Yes," Gerdty chuckled "and she has a thirst for social justice, too."

Susie nodded. "I can explain the texts when Viisi reads for me but it's hard to concentrate when I'm in pain. Please help?" And with that, the air shimmered and the dragon crouched humbly on the ground in her true form, huge wings drooping, horned head bowed.

"How can I apply medications without fresh plant materials?" Gerdty sighed, waving her arm toward the garden.

"I will help you."

"Well, Susie. Dragons are wiser and do greater magic than I dreamt of."

"Please, can you not call me Susie? My name is Shoshan. It means 'lily' in the Hebrew language. I was born during King Solomon's reign."

"Oh my," said Gerdty, calculating that that meant the dragon was three thousand years old.

Shoshan groaned as she stretched. "I am old and tired

now, disoriented and blind. It seems I can't move without wreaking havoc, but I don't damage anything intentionally. Can you help me?"

"Okay," agreed Gerdty, exhaling with finality. She recognized symptoms of ill health in her human patients. Wasn't Susie just another old woman whose fire waned? Catching the glow of the setting sun on the dragon's stained teeth, Gerdty promised, "Your discomfort can be cured with time, patience, and good work done by both of us."

Shoshan opened her huge mouth and allowed Gerdty to reach in with head and hands, and deftly apply thymol disinfectant. With a soft-bristled brush, Gerdty spread myrrh on Shoshan's swollen, aching gums. Shoshan smiled in relief before drifting off to sleep.

***

Gerdty treated her patient regularly over the following days, applying thymol and myrrh after carefully brushing her teeth with cleansing hyssop, and massaging gums and jaw muscles with dexterous fingers. Using borrowed blacksmith's tongs, Gerdty extracted a goat horn stuck at the back of Shoshan's mouth, the source of infection and agony.

"Huzzah!" Gerdty exclaimed. "One tormentor is gone!"

They cackled like old hens, amused at how simple relief could come. The traditional healer could teach college-trained dentist Milly Stevenson about patient care!

The dragon convalesced beneath spreading trees beside a gurgling stream at the far end of our farm, secluded yet within hearing and sight from our house. I checked on her before leaving on Monday for my rounds of butchery, and after returning with the setting sun on Friday, bringing venison to share with our guest.

Marianne discovered Susie grazing with my Holsteins one morning when she collected them from the pasture for milking.

"Hello," growled the dragon, smiling jaggedly. "What are you singing?"

"Good morning to you," replied Marianne, politely bowing. "It's 'Early One Morning,' a lament about lost love."

"I like your bittersweet love song."

Marianne was astonished that such a terrifying creature could speak pleasantly and graze among livestock that showed no concern she might eat them.

The dragon basked in the sunlight, blithely watching cows follow the milkmaid. She smiled when Gerdty marched toward her, carrying toothbrush and medicine bucket to administer morning oral care.

Marianne came daily to do farm chores, and Shoshan joined in her songs.

At Gerdty's instruction, the maid brought fresh carrots as food to improve Susie's eyesight and willow bark to chew for pain.

In return, the dragon helped Marianne plough and weed Gerdty's new garden patch. She was happy in her sanctuary, relieved to not kill or burn to protect herself from superstitious people.

"Someday," she told Marianne, "I will share my dragon song with you, but not yet."

***

Marianne excitedly told Jack McCready of Shoshan's promise. He told his lover, Princess Viisi, that a talking, singing dragon resided at the butcher's farm.

Viisi slipped from the castle. She met Jack, and they rode on horseback to Gerdty and Roland's farm. A thick wisdom book from her father's library bounced in her saddlebag. They tied their horses at the hitching rail, then Jack set Princess Viisi's saddlebag over his shoulder and they joined Gerdty and me to cross the pasture to where the dragon dozed.

"Greetings, Shoshan," called Princess Viisi.

"Greetings," rumbled Shoshan, a dark mass but for her eyes and teeth glistening in the moon beams.

"I hope that you are well? Marianne told me you are well cared for here by Roland and Gerdty."

The dragon stretched open her wings and settled them again upon her back. "Yes, I'm recovering splendidly and will soon return to my mountain."

"I am happy for you."

"Thank you, but tell me," blinked the dragon, "how goes your campaign to unseat Mayor Sanchez and best Dr. Stevenson?"

Viisi glanced at Jack who pulled a book and handed it to her.

"I borrowed *Wisdom Literature* from my father's library. It's attributed to King Solomon himself. This is a Latin translation of his proverbs."

"Sit on my shoulder, where I can hear the sage voice of Solomon come alive from such a bright young scholar," invited Shoshan.

Unfolding one of her great wings onto the ground for the princess to ride, the dragon smoothly lifted her up. Viisi laughed, thrilled at her lofty elevation, and waved gaily to her friends watching in amazement from far below.

"I read to Father today at breakfast. He was intrigued, and promised to mentor me well, should I become mayor."

"He should mentor you regardless," said Shoshan. "Yours is a mind that deserves to be honed."

Susie mentioned other insightful texts, written by other philosophers in different times. "Your mediaeval backwater could benefit from rediscovering such creativity, but I digress...

"As a king's daughter and a budding leader of people, please remember Lady Wisdom's enduring importance. I can tutor you as long as my health revives and I have sanctuary, so feel free to confide in me," concluded Shoshan with a yawn. "But now it is time for sleep. Goodnight."

I wrapped my arms around my wife and Jack held Princess Viisi's hand. We murmured optimistically about the good things to come in Zos.

***

It was hard to hide a dragon.

Sanchez and Milly declared that *our* evil dragon continued to destroy property, devour children and livestock, and caused the economy to stagnate.

When Princess Viisi challenged such lies at a political rally, her rivals vilified her for protecting the enemy, and accused Gerdty and me of pampering a monster.

I was called a traitor, and Gerdty was called a witch!

One morning Marianne burst through the door during breakfast, shrieking that a mob was coming to kill Shoshan and raze our farm.

Marianne howled, "What should we do?"

"We can't reason with madmen, and we don't have means to fight them," I said, watching from the window as the hostile column marched closer. "We should hide in the king's forests while his troops disband this mob."

"We're not leaving without Shoshan," said Gerdty.

"How?"

"Marianne, hitch up the cart to the mules. Roland, go get Shoshan. Tell her to transform into a girl. If anyone confronts us on the road, explain that we are taking our new maid to the market today. Go quickly! Marianne, help

Roland. I'll gather up some things, and then join you. We'll leave by the back gate."

I explained this plan to Shoshan with a pitchfork in my hand, gesturing to the wagon as Marianne raced to bridle the mules.

"Stop worrying, both of you," advised Shoshan. "I know we are all in danger. We don't have time to prepare mules and wagon, nor are human plans necessary. I can fly you to any sanctuary."

"Our enemies will shoot you down," Marianne groaned.

"Dragons are magical as well as wise and mighty, remember?" Shoshan winked her fierce eye. "Now I'm healthy, I can make myself and anyone who rides on my back invisible. I fly higher than anything fired by catapult, cannon, or archer. I can fly above clouds, among the stars, or skim tree tops or ground. Let's get Gerdty."

She gave us a low-altitude test run to the yard where my applauding wife and her bulging sack awaited. Squatting by the house, Shoshan brought Gerdty aboard.

Within a blink of an eye, we disappeared into the sky, disguised.

The approaching mob didn't acknowledge the

majestic eagle as it soared above them.

Sanchez, Milly Mandible, and their savage minions found our farm vacant, save for a few cows docilely chewing their cud and two mules eyeing them from the pasture.

From above we watched as the crowd set our house ablaze.

A bright light flashed at the fork of two empty roads.

"It's Jack, signalling us by hand mirror," said Marianne. She shimmied up the dragon's neck and called into her ear, "Let us down there."

The dragon complied, as she transformed again into an eagle. Upon the ground, we were transformed back to ourselves before an astonished Jack.

He joined us on Shoshan's back and then we transformed again into an eagle. We followed the trail of woodsmen and hunters toward jagged, snow-covered mountain peaks that guarded the borders of the kingdom.

We spotted another light flashing from higher up, and by late afternoon, met Viisi standing watch while her horse grazed nearby.

The eagle spiralled downward until it landed in a meadow. It hopped toward the spellbound princess, but then transformed into the golden dragon.

"I'm so glad you made the journey safely!" marvelled Viisi, as she hugged the humans and rubbed affectionately the horned head of the exhausted dragon.

Viisi quickly escorted us along a secret trail. Adding to the eeriness of the silent forest, Shoshan glided above us like a protective shadow.

We entered a large clearing. Shelter pavilions painted to match the forest had cots with soft pillows and warm blankets. Chopped wood and kindling were stacked in a frame. A sharp axe and a flint hung from the support pole. Labels on a collection of barrels indicated they contained wine, bread, vegetables, cured meat, or fresh water.

A cookfire crackled a welcome.

I exclaimed at the quality of the provisions and shelter.

Viisi laughed. "The king himself chose this sanctuary for you. I confess even I did not expect it would still be so luxuriously furnished. We came here as a family on summer picnics when I was a child. It is a secure place. I must return to the castle, but you are safe here. Please relax."

***

We did the princess's bidding and enjoyed our sanctuary.

Marianne caught fish and drew water from creeks encountered during daily walkabouts.

Gerdty brewed healing teas from chamomile, comfrey and veronica to help Shoshan's rheumatism or asthma.

Dragon and healer also ventured onto the meadow during sunny mornings, where Shoshan unfurled as a dragon among adoring faeries, and let Gerdty administer aloe vera, gentian violet and guaiacum to flaky scales on her back.

They foraged together for medicinal plants like wild mint, wintergreen, thyme, gentian, dragon's bane, sassafras, juniper, and fir to replenish Gerdty's depleted medicine chest and garden. They cut leaves, seeds, flowers, or roots to dry in the sun, then placed them in cloth pouches and put them into the sack for transport home.

After chores were completed, Marianne and Shoshan serenaded us with duets.

One placid afternoon as everyone lounged at the forest edge, Shoshan said, "It is time. I would share my special song with you."

We all sat up, aware of the great honour.

Marianne sighed, "I wish I had my lute to accompany your song."

Shoshan shook her great head. "This is a song I sing just for you. You must find your own songs to share."

Then she sang to us of the joy of flight, the losses of long life, the power of her purpose, her gratitude for her place in the universe.

We were awed and humbled at the beauty and power of her song, but even if we wished to, we could not repeat it. Human throats are not formed to create dragon song.

***

The next day, Princess Viisi and King George arrived with a train of men, court advisors, and horses to escort us back to the castle.

"Greet your new mayor!" the king announced, beaming at his daughter.

We congratulated her with whoops of joy.

Shoshan had transformed into a human girl again, and she and Viisi danced down the trail, laughing together like old friends.

"*That* lovely girl cavorting with my daughter is a

dragon?" the king wondered to me.

"Aye, sire. Shoshan is a magical creature who blesses everyone."

Gerdty joined us and added, "Now she has been healed, our village will prosper under the influence of her magic."

"Indeed," he acknowledged. "We had no idea the influence she had until her illness deprived us of the harmony we had so long enjoyed."

As the royal train descended the mountains, Viisi explained the changes to come.

"I expect those who caused trouble to contribute honourably to society. Dr. Sanchez and his followers are to build Roland and Gerdty a new house. Milly Stevenson will be our dentist but she will study professional ethics and Dr. Sanchez will supervise to ensure her practice to be honest and fair."

"No more stealing wisdom teeth?" I asked.

"Precisely. Folks can keep their wisdom. Tell them our other idea, Father."

The king grinned broadly. "I have agreed to open the knowledge vault. Scientists and labourers alike may come to ponder apt wisdom of their ancestors."

As we entered into the streets of Zos, cheering crowds waved as their king and mayor paraded by. With just as much enthusiasm they applauded Marianne, Gerdty and me.

We could hear the murmurs as spectators saw the beautiful woman riding beside Princess Viisi. They had not the slightest inkling they were viewing a dragon in human form.

That afternoon we were treated to baths and new clothing.

Come evening, at trumpet-heralded invitation, the villagers filled the castle for a sumptuous feast.

Both royals and commoners made speeches of congratulation and anticipation, lauding achievements made and to come.

Princess Viisi rose to her feet and the crowd grew silent. "I give thanks for Shoshan, a dragon we called Susie. She is the catalyst who inspired the community to seek better days.

"She is a dragon – our friend, not a problem," declared Viisi. "I am thankful that Shoshan chooses to dwell peacefully among us. As mayor and daughter of your king, I proclaim that she is always welcome here in Zos. She is integral to the community's social fabric." She raised her glass and declared, "To Shoshan!"

In deafening chorus, the crowd responded, "To Shoshan!"

The beautiful woman rose to her feet. "Thank you, my friends, for this declaration. I am confident that we all will flourish." She turned to Princess Viisi and added, "Should you have need of me, you have only to flash your light to my mountain."

Then, before the astonished eyes of the villagers, she assumed her dragon form. She unfolded her huge wings and flew majestically into the moonlight.

IF YOU ENJOYED THIS BOOK

PLEASE LEAVE A REVIEW

AT YOUR FAVOURITE SITE! THANK YOU!

DRAGON WRANGLERS:

wherein

the reader learns

about some interesting writers

Patricia L. Atchison lives in a small city in central Alberta, nurturing a nest of gold dragon eggs. While searching for a rare blue sapphire one, Patricia writes children's picture books, and young adult and inspirational stories which she shares on her Substack.com newsletter, The Write Flavor. She finished writing a young adult fantasy duology which she hopes will soon soar across open horizons.

Bonny Beswick, born, raised and living in southern Alberta, loves to travel the seven seas in search of dragons.

She is a self-published author. Her first novel, Under the Ombu Tree, is an historical romance set on the Argentine pampas (no, there are no dragons). Current projects include a sequel to her first book, and a police-procedural murder mystery set in Calgary, Alberta. Bonny also loves to write short stories, and sooner or later, there be dragons featured!

Isabel Cave did not start life in Canada. She was born in Stratford-Upon-Avon where she lived until she was four, when her family moved to Bath. As a result, she grew up with Shakespeare and Jane Austen and was therefore destined to see lots of plays and hoard books in her lair. Isabel has a long-suffering husband and three children who often send out search parties to bookshops when she sneaks off in search of treasure.

She also has a clan of cats and a loyal hound who accompany her on many adventures. Isabel has an MA in Creative Writing and writes poetry and mystical tales.

Abby Duncan is originally from British Columbia. She is an author and technophile who now resides in Southern Alberta. She and her husband are caretakers of a tiny luck dragon who guards their home, and, most importantly, his hoard of toys.

Kelly Komm has a "day job," but covets her Book Dragon alter ego as she prowls the bookstores of Edmonton for additions to her hoard. Her literary life thus far has included publishing fantasy fiction, poetry, and short stories. For a few years, she guided elementary students through the NaNoWriMo Young Writer's Program. She has dabbled in editing, and in creating book trailers.

Other than creating from the point of view of The Wind, Kelly has been having a blast collaborating on a childrens' sci-fi graphic novel.

Kathleen Ladislaus dabbles in writing fantasy and paranormal tales. An avid amateur genealogist, you'll find some of her characters named after an ancestor or two. Books have always been a joy for her; writing is a natural extension of that and has become a passion. Perennially curious, her musings and research on real world issues are woven into her novels. Above all, she likes a good story, and is happiest when writing stories to share with you, the reader and any dragons who may be eavesdropping.

Alison McBain's novels are the recipients of over 13 awards, and her short work has been published in *On Spec, Abyss & Apex*, and *Flash Fiction Online*, among other magazines. She's currently pursuing a project called "Author Versus AI," where she's writing a book a week over the course of a year, using NO AI at all (52 books total). When not writing, Ms. McBain is associate editor for the magazine *ScribesMICRO* and draws dragons all over the walls of her house with the enthusiastic help of her kids. She lives near Edmonton, Alberta.

Robert Proudfoot, from Edmonton, published: *Enduring Art, Active Faith* (poetry, short stories, essays, and artwork), plus an audiobook; *A Playful Policeman Meets the Citizen-making Teacher* (biographical sketch of Robert's grandparents); *Come By Here, My Lord* (coming-of-age novel, where friendships develop across racial barriers in southern Africa during 1970s apartheid/colonial era); and *Amateurs on Safari* (1970 memoir about camping across East Africa). Robert is currently writing sequels to *Come By Here, My Lord*, plus short stories that speculate how troubled people might obtain help from poignant experiences or supernatural forces. May dragons' ancient magic heal today's suffering world.

Halli Reid is a purveyor of curiosities, a hoarder of books, an enthusiast of nightmares, and a smith of spoken words. The manifestation of her physical form resides within the Bridge of Leth with her triple relevant offspring and triple feline familiars. In another reality, Halli is a linguist and a pirate, sailing the shores of ancient alliterations, plundering dialects and discussions. She chides children for their tripping tongues and late literacy and expensive expressions. She remedies the unreasonable, softens the suffering and empowers the emancipated.

Mafalda Rose is proudly a part of Team Dragon, a lifelong resident of Calgary and an admirer of all creatures spiky and scaled. Prior to her chapter in *The Dragon Problem*, she had a poem published for the Poetry Institute of Canada in 2016. Now, she works on various different stories, ranging from short horror stories to a historical fantasy currently at ten thousand words, when her work isn't interrupted by life or cats.

NEW SPACES:

an anthology of sci-fi short stories

Within your mind and across the universe, there are new spaces to explore!

From Lintusen Press comes this collection of ten science fiction short stories from authors Finnian Burnett, Andrew G. Cooper, J. Paul Cooper, BC Deeks, Nancy Kilpatrick, Philip Mann, Lee F. Patrick, Halli Reid, KT Wagner, and Jarrod K. Williams.

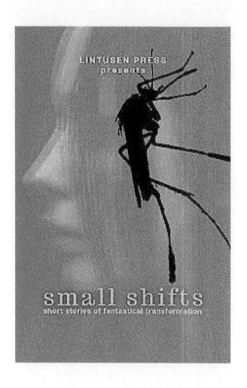

SMALL SHIFTS:

short stories of fantastical transformation

Not all shifters turn into magnificent beasts. Sure, there are those humans who transform into wolves and bears, but this book is about the smaller creatures. Learn about the trials and tribulations of folks who turn into raccoons, hamsters, mosquitoes, or bumblebees. 11 delightful tales of Small Shifts.

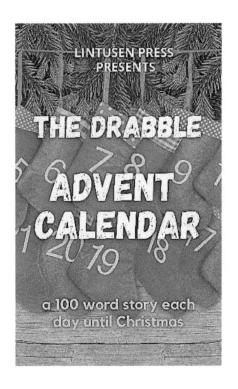

THE DRABBLE ADVENT CALENDAR

A drabble is a story of precisely one hundred words. Here are 25 family friendly winter themed drabbles; one perfectly complete tidbit of story to savour each day leading up to Christmas

Please visit

LintusenPress.com

to learn more about our upcoming releases

and to see submission calls

for our future publications.

Milton Keynes UK
Ingram Content Group UK Ltd.
UKHW030319090824
446663UK00001B/37